G000124881

TURN OF THE TIDE

TURN OF THE TIDE

Elizabeth Jeffrey

Illustrated by Graham Gurr

CANONGATE

First published in 1989 by
Canongate Publishing Limited
17 Jeffrey Street, Edinburgh

© Elizabeth Jeffrey, 1989
© illustrations Graham Gurr

British Library Cataloguing in Publication Data
Jeffrey, Elizabeth
Turn of the tide.
I. Title
823'.914[J]

ISBN 0-86241-237-4

Typeset by Hewer Text Composition Services, Edinburgh
Printed and bound in Great Britain
by Billings & Son Ltd, Worcester

To four very special young people;
my grandchildren,
Rachael, Benjamin, Jessica and Matthew.

CONTENTS

THE MEETING

Jan cowered between two barrels as the blows rained down on him.

'You little varmit, I'll teach you to steal my apples,' the swarthy stall-holder yelled, grabbing him by the ear and pulling him out.

'Leggo my ear!' Jan dealt the stall-holder a smart crack on the shin with his clog, but this only served to enrage the man further and the blows began to rain down even harder.

Then, out of the corner of his eye, Jan saw a quick movement from the crowd as a boy of about the same age as himself dashed up to the apple barrow and in a swift movement pulled out the iron pegs that held up the end.

It was early morning in the market. The stall-holder had brought a good, full load of fresh, ripe apples in from the country to sell and they were piled, red and juicy, high on his barrow. At least, they had been piled high. Now, as the end swung down they cascaded on to the road like a red sea; a red sea that turned green and then to brown as the unripe and rotten apples hidden underneath came to light.

With an oath the stall-holder released Jan's ear, for a split second undecided whether to grab the other boy or rescue his stock of apples.

The boy made the decision for him. He grabbed Jan's hand and with a 'Quick, this way. Follow me,' he dived into the crowd of people thronging the market.

Jan followed as he dodged between the stalls of fruit and vegetables, the piles of pots and pans and baskets and other household goods, not to mention the squawking chickens and geese, until, at the edge of the market he ran down a narrow alleyway and stopped.

'We can't stay here,' the boy said breathlessly speaking in English, half to himself, 'we'll have half Amsterdam after us.'

'Come with me, then. I know a place,' Jan replied, also in English. 'Oh, don't look so surprised. I may look Dutch but my mother is English. Come on, this way.' He led the way through twisting streets and alleyways and over narrow canal bridges, often doubling back on himself to make sure they were not followed. But people in Amsterdam in the year 1572 had more urgent things to worry about than a pair of young apple thieves. For this was a time of intrigue and war, with the whole of the Netherlands in revolt against their Ruler, Philip of Spain, the notorious Catholic king. Under his orders the cruel and tyrannical Duke of Alva was leading an army to crush state after state in the name of religion. Only those of the Catholic faith were spared; the rest were tortured and massacred in their thousands, some without any chance to defend themselves. No wonder non-Catholics were fleeing to Protestant England — some escaping in such a hurry that they arrived with little more than the clothes they stood up in.

Eventually the two boys reached the waterfront and Jan slipped through a doorway into a large wooden building. It looked as if it was used for a fisherman's store, and smelled like it, too, with old crates and lobster pots littering the floor and fishing nets hung from the eaves to dry. Jan led the way up the rickety stairs to the loft above. Here, there were a few more lobster pots, mostly broken, some sacks and a heap of straw.

'We'll be safe enough here,' he said. 'I've lived here for a week and no one's found me yet.' He turned to his companion. 'My name's Jan de Hane. I haven't thanked you properly yet for rescuing me from that old man.' He surveyed his bruises. 'You wouldn't have thought he'd have missed *one* apple, would you?' he said ruefully.

'I'm Nicholas Piper, but everyone calls me Nick.' The English boy was reaching inside his jerkin as he spoke and now he brought out apple after rosy apple, each one bigger and juicier-looking than the last. 'I can see you're not very used to this game, Jan,' he said with a grin, biting into one and letting the juice run down his chin, leaving a clean mark. 'The thing to do if you want to help yourself is to create a diversion, didn't you know that?'

'No,' Jan said thoughtfully, following suit and picking up an apple. 'I'm not used to this kind of life at all. And to tell you the truth I don't like it much.' He looked at the apple in his hand. 'This is the first thing I'll have eaten for two days.' He took a large bite.

Nick looked interested. 'What are you doing here, in Amsterdam, then?'

'I'm looking for a way to get my mother and sister to England.'

'Where are they?'

'At home. We live in a little village about three days walk from here. I've left them a note to say where I've gone. If my mother had known what I intended to do she would have stopped me so I didn't tell her.'

'Why? Doesn't she want to leave? From the dreadful stories I've heard I should've thought she'd have been only too glad to get out of this country.'

'Yes, but you see we've no money to pay for a passage. So I thought that if I could somehow smuggle myself to England I

11

could perhaps find my English relatives and get them to pay to bring my mother and sister over.'

'Who are your mother's relatives? And where do they live?'

'That's just it, I don't know. My mother never talks about them. All I know is that her family were furious when she wanted to marry my father. A Dutch sea captain was not the husband they had in mind for her. So she ran away with him and after they were married they came to live in Holland.'

Nick stroked his chin. 'Ain't you got *anything* to go on? Any clue at all as to where she came from?'

'Not really. Only the fact that if she fell in love with a sea captain the chances are she lived near the sea.'

'Is that all?'

Jan puckered his face. 'She never talked about her family. After the accident I wanted her to write to them and ask for help, but she flew into such a rage that I never ever dared mention it again.'

'What accident?' Nick began on his third apple.

'A coach my parents were travelling in overturned. My father was thrown clear but he struck his head and was killed outright. My mother was trapped inside the coach and ever since her legs have been funny. She can't walk much, even with crutches.' Jan picked up another apple and polished it slowly on his shirt. 'We used to live in quite a nice house with a garden and a servant but after the accident we had to move to a pokey little cottage and my mother had to spin and sew to keep us.' He bit into the apple. 'It's not very easy to find people who want spinning done these days. They're all leaving the country.'

'You can't blame them for that,' Nick remarked. 'I wouldn't want to stay here for long. You never know when you might find yourself with your throat slit or roasting gently alive.' He shuddered. 'No, thank you. The sooner I get back to England the better.'

'That's why I want to get my mother and sister away,' Jan said. 'If they fall into the hands of Alva's Papish barbarians heaven knows what might become of them.'

'Don't you know *anything* else?' Nick persisted.

Jan shook his head sadly. Then he brightened up. 'Oh, yes.' He felt inside his shirt and brought out a scrap of paper. 'I tore this out of my mother's Bible. She told me once, a long time ago, that this was where she used to live.' He handed Nick the paper. On it was drawn a large half-timbered house, heavily pargeted on the upper storey and under the eaves. Worked into the ornate plaster-work were, unmistakably, the initials JCR.

Nick handed it back. 'Thass not a lot to go on,' he said gloomily.

'No, but it's *something*. If only I could get to England . . .' Jan's voice trailed off. 'But nobody wants a cabin boy and every time I try to stow away I get caught and thrown off. You wouldn't think they'd even notice me among all those people down there on the quay, would you?' He got up and walked over to a chink in the wall.

Below was the wharf where boats were being loaded and unloaded with much banging and clattering and shouting of directions. Vats of silver herrings glinted in the June sunlight, adding a distinctive smell to the overall stench of tarred rope, unwashed bodies and rotting vegetation that rose on the hot summer air.

Nick followed him. 'I s'pose I could smuggle you on to my ship,' he said thoughtfully. He frowned. 'But if Captain Harvey found out he'd never have me aboard again.

'Where is your ship?'

'Over there, look, the *Mimosa*, next to those old fishing smacks.' He pointed to a small square-rigged ketch, lying along-side the quay.

'Where do you come from?'

'Colchester. On the east coast of England, on the River Colne.

'Colchester,' Jan repeated. 'It sounds like part of the word on my lucky charm.' He fished inside his shirt and brought out a kind of medallion, fastened round his neck with a leather thong. 'Look, it says 1550DUTYS COLCESTERJ and then some more letter I can't read. That looks like an L and an N and a G or a CS at the end.'

Nick looked, but without much interest. He wasn't going to admit to Jan that letters meant almost nothing to a boy who could neither read nor write. 'Where'd you get it from?' he asked.

'I found it in a box when we moved house. My mother said it had belonged to her brother Richard. He was killed in a riding accident when he was seventeen. She said it hadn't brought her much luck so I could have it if I wanted it.'

Nick turned it over and saw three crowns with a cross imprinted on it. 'Has it brought you any luck so far?'

Jan gave his new friend a playful punch. 'I suppose you could say it brought you to my rescue,' he grinned. 'And if you'll smuggle me aboard your ship . . .'

'I didn't say I'd do that. I said I most probably *could*. But I'm not sure. I'll have to think about it. If I want to be a ship's captain one day I can't afford to get on the wrong side of Captain Harvey. He says he'll help me.' He swelled with pride.

'Is that what you want to do? Be a ship's captain?' Jan asked.

'Yes. I'd really like to join the Royal Navy and sail all over the world, instead of back and forth between Colchester and Amsterdam like I do now.' Nick went to the head of the rickety stairs. 'Our ship sails tomorrow, on the tide. I'll come and see you tonight, after dark, and tell you if I've managed to arrange anything for you.' With a wave he disappeared from sight.

Jan settled himself on the heap of sacks to wait. He was still hungry, the apples didn't seem to have helped much, in fact they'd made him feel hungrier than ever. But he didn't feel inclined to risk any more cuffs and punches by going out to try and steal more food and he'd no money to buy any. What little money he'd brought with him from home had been used up in the first few days, most of it on bribing a seaman to smuggle him aboard his ship at dusk. But when dusk came the seaman, the ship and Jan's money were all on the high seas and Jan had been left penniless on the shore.

He wondered if the same thing would happen with Nick. Somehow, he didn't think so, but if it did he wouldn't have lost anything because he hadn't given him anything. He fingered the lucky charm round his neck. Funny that the letters on the charm should sound so much like Colchester, where Nick came from. Perhaps it was an omen. A good omen. Still fingering the charm he closed his eyes and fell asleep.

It was twilight when he woke and Nick was standing over him. Jan struggled up on one elbow. 'I didn't hear you come up,' he said, rubbing his eyes.

'I've learned to move quiet,' Nick told him. He squatted down beside him. 'I've come to tell you I can't do it,' he said, coming straight to the point. 'Thass no good, I can't smuggle you aboard without telling the Captain, it wouldn't be right. He's like a father to me now my gran's dead. I'm sorry, Jan.'

Jan hung his head. 'If you gave me a sign it was clear I could stow myself away,' he mumbled.

Nick thought for a minute. Then he shook his head. 'No, because I'd still know what you were up to. I'm sorry, Jan, and I wish you luck. I only wish I could 'elp you.'

'Couldn't you *ask* Captain Harvey?' Jan pleaded.

'I know it wouldn't be any good. He's already got more refugees than the ship can safely take. I did ask him if he could use another cabin boy, Jan, but he boxed my ears and said he'd got more than he needed already.' Nick turned to go. 'I came to tell you, Jan, I didn't just want to sail off and leave you wondering.'

'Thanks. It was kind of you.' Jan's voice was barely a mumble now, he was so bitterly disappointed.

Suddenly, a door opened below them and three men came in, half-carrying a fourth between them as he struggled to escape. The boys, with one accord, dropped on their stomachs and edged forward to the edge of the loft to see what was happening. As his hat fell off they could see that the fourth man had a long, ugly scar running the length of his cheek, from his temple till it disappeared into his beard somewhere in the region of his chin. They watched

15

as one of the three men tied Scarface's hands behind his back and secured him to one of the wooden pillars that supported the loft where the boys were hidden.

'Now, will you speak!' said one, holding a knife to Scarface's throat.

'I have nothing to say,' Scarface said quietly.

'He's English,' Jan whispered. 'I'm sure of it. He speaks Dutch with a heavy accent.'

'Two of the others have got knives. The other one's got a pistol,' Nick pointed out, 'so if we jump down and startle them we'll only end up getting carved up or shot ourselves.'

The first man stepped back into the shadows with the others. It was impossible for the boys to see what was going on because of the fishing nets that were draped from the roof so they crawled a little nearer the edge of the loft.

'What's it all about? Can you hear what they're saying?' Nick asked.

Jan put a finger to his mouth and cocked his ear. 'They're trying to decide whether to kill him outright or whether it's worthwhile trying to torture information out of him,' he whispered after a few minutes. 'Oh, poor man, they're going to cut off his fingers and thumbs . . .'

'Quick, then, afore they move. While they're all standing in a group. Undo the rope on that cleat by your elbow the minute I say NOW. See it? Thass right, that one, there. NOW!'

Swiftly, Jan did as Nick had bidden him, while Nick moved round to the other side and uncleated the rope there. As the rope sagged the fishing nets collapsed round the three men, enmeshing them in a slimy, wet, evil-smelling tangle that only trapped them more as they tried to escape from it.

As the boys shinned down the nearest pillar and took Scarface's dagger from his belt to cut him free, the man with the pistol fired a shot but it went wide.

'This way,' Jan called, wriggling between the tar barrels and lobster pots to a space at the far end of the shed where the boarding was loose. He prised out two loose nails and swung

16

open a hole big enough for them to climb through although it was a bit of a squeeze for Scarface. Then he replaced the boards and the nails.

'Whew!' Scarface dusted himself down. 'That was a bit of a near thing. I was beginning to wonder how I was going to get myself out of that little party. Thank you, my young friends.' He looked at the two boys. They were both about the same age, he judged, about twelve or thirteen years old. One was fair, with frank blue eyes and a serious, rather apprehensive expression. The other boy was darker, with a ready smile and darting brown eyes that missed nothing. There was not an ounce of spare flesh on either of them and they were rather grubby, with clothes that looked as if they'd seen better days. He guessed, rightly, that they were hungry. He put his hand to his mouth in an eating gesture. 'Hungry?' he asked, in English.

Both boys nodded vigorously. 'Starving!' they both said together.

Scarface raised his eyebrows in surprise. 'You're English?'

'I am,' Nick said. He jabbed a finger towards Jan. 'He ain't. But he speaks English all right.'

'Then what in thunder are you doing in this place?' The man frowned. 'But never mind that now. The first thing is to get you fed.'

A quayside inn where there were plenty of people seemed the safest place to go and there Scarface ordered an enormous dish of fish stew to be brought, from which they could replenish their plates as they became empty. Jan had four platefuls, Nick had five and while they ate Scarface made notes — a series of dots made by denting the paper with the point of his knife.

'There,' he said when he had finished, folding it up and putting it in his pouch. 'Now even if it falls into the wrong hands it won't give anything away. But what I need more than anything is to get to England. And fast.'

Nick looked up, his usually pale face rosy from the hot stew, 'My ship sails on tomorrow's tide. But my captain . . .'

'Will you take me to him?'

'I'm sorry. He says he can't take any more . . .'

Scarface waved his hand. 'You just take me to him, my young friend. It's surprising how the sight of gold can make room for an extra man. I can pay, and pay well for a swift and safe passage. Amsterdam is not the healthiest place for a man in my profession to be in at the moment.'

'What is your profession?' Jan asked eagerly.

Scarface looked at him for a moment and then gave a lopsided smile. 'Shall we just say that I work for the . . .' he broke off and a look of alarm crossed his face. 'Quick, is there a back entrance? I think we might be safer elsewhere.'

Jan and Nick looked round. Three men had just come in, the three who had held Scarface prisoner. They looked in an ugly mood as they questioned the landlord.

It was fortunate that Scarface and the two boys were in a small room off the main bar. They slipped over to the window and Scarface dropped the boys over the sill one at a time then climbed out himself.

'I do feel,' he said, clamping his hat back on his head, 'that the sooner I'm on board a ship bound for England the safer I'll be. Please, my young friend, take me to your captain. Now. Before anything else happens.'

'You'd better wait here, Jan,' Nick said, when they reached the *Mimosa*, which didn't smell nearly as sweet as her name implied.

'But . . .' Jan protested.

Nick dropped behind Scarface. 'I did tell you that I couldn't help you,' he said sadly. 'I'm sorry, Jan, truly I am. But I'll tell you what I'll do. I'll see if I can find out anything about your family. I promise I will. And I'll be back here in about three weeks. I'll see you then and tell you what I've been able to discover.'

Jan turned away. 'Some friend you've turned out to be,' he said bitterly. 'When does your ship sail?'

'As soon as the last of those fleeces are aboard. They were brought here by mistake on another boat. Captain Harvey is

18

taking them back. He's not pleased, I can tell you, at having to handle such a stinking cargo.'

Scarface turned round. 'Come on, lad, time's pressing. Say goodbye to your Dutch friend and take me aboard.' He came back a few steps and pressed a gold coin into Jan's hand. 'There, my young friend. That'll buy you many a fish stew, with my thanks. Goodbye, now, and thanks for your assistance.'

'Goodbye, Jan,' Nick said. 'I'll see you when I come back.'

But Jan had turned away to hide his tears of disappointment. What was he to do now? He daren't go home because who could tell how far the Spanish army had advanced by now? They would think nothing of killing a boy alone on the road. And what of his mother and Betkin? If he couldn't get them to England what would their fate be?

He looked desperately around at the sea of masts. Surely one of these boats could take him across the German Sea to England so that he could look for his grandfather. A seaman jostled past him, swearing in a foreign tongue and fear clutched at Jan's heart. Suppose he stowed away on the wrong boat! He could end up in the wrong country!

The tears began to flow again. Oh, what was he to do? He had never felt so alone and helpless in the whole of his life.

PASSAGE TO ENGLAND

Jan watched dejectedly as the men loaded the fleeces on to the *Mimosa*. They were going as deck cargo because the holds were full. Each man hefted a fleece on to his shoulder and carried it up the gangplank to add to the growing heap on top of the already battened hatches. Some of the fleeces weren't bundled all that tightly. . . .

Almost before the idea had formed in his mind Jan took a deep breath and dived into the middle of the most loosely-bound fleece, using his fingers to make an air-hole for himself. The stench was awful but as he felt himself lifted high in the air and flung down on the deck he didn't care. He was on board the *Mimosa*. Soon he would be in England!

It wasn't long before he realised he'd made a ghastly mistake. The heat inside the fleece was stifling and his little air-hole barely kept him from suffocating. It was only the fact that his fleece, purely by lucky chance, was stacked on a corner that was saving him from an early death. But he daren't wriggle free whilst there

20

was so much activity on deck, he knew he must wait until it was dark and the ship well under way. Then he would be able to stretch his cramped legs and breathe fresh air for a while. Beyond that he had no thought.

Carefully, he worked his air-hole a little bigger so that he could see something through the thick wool and also breathe a bit more easily. The deck seemed to be swarming with people. He didn't know whether to be glad or sorry. Among so many people surely another one wouldn't be noticed. On the other hand it meant more eyes and voices to raise a hue and cry. Then everything went black as a huge canvas was thrown over the fleeces and ropes secured it to the deck. Now there was no escape and precious little air. The stink from the fleeces began to make him feel sick. He just hoped he wouldn't take too long to die. . . .

To his surprise he was still alive some hours later. He knew by the gentle roll of the ship that they were at sea but he had no way of knowing whether it was night or day in the stinking woolly blackness. Suddenly, he felt a draught of cool, fresh air and Nick's voice whispered, 'Jan, are you there? Can you wriggle out?'

Jan clawed his way out of his tight cocoon inch by inch. Nick had loosened the rope at the corner of the canvas just enough for him to crawl out on to the deck and the two boys huddled together, hidden in the shadows between the pile of fleeces and the main mast.

'That was a good thing I saw you dive into that fleece,' Nick said sternly. 'If I hadn't, you'd have been finished by the time we reached Colchester.'

'I thought I was finished anyway,' Jan gasped, taking great gulps of the sweet night air.

'Look, I've brought you some water. I couldn't manage any food, but I don't suppose you're hungry.'

'No, I'm not. And neither would you be if you'd been squashed in those horrible fleeces. Ugh, I feel sick.'

21

'You can't be sick,' Nick ordered. 'And you'll have to get used to the fleeces.' He stuck his head under the canvas. 'Yuk, I see what you mean,' he said, pulling it out quickly. 'But you'll have to stay there, Jan. There's not an inch of space anywhere on the ship where I could hide you better. I'll bring you food and water whenever I can, I promise you that.' He grinned, his teeth showing white in the darkness. 'I'm glad you managed to smuggle yourself aboard. I hated the thought of leaving you behind on the quay, Jan.'

Nick was as good as his word. Every night he brought Jan water and food and kept watch while he eased his cramped muscles on deck. Fortunately the crossing was smooth and apart from one fearful hour when powerful sailors came and checked the ropes on the deck cargo, forcing Jan to burrow deep in the fleeces to avoid discovery, uneventful.

When they were off Brightlingsea Nick came to him and told him to get ready to leave the ship.

'That couldn't have worked better,' he whispered, crouching beside where Jan lay concealed. 'Captain Harvey is anxious to be rid of Scarface before we reach the docks at Colchester so he's ordered me to set him ashore at Wyvenhoe and I'll be able to put you ashore there, too.' He leaned a bit closer. 'Scarface is an important man, Jan, but I ain't been able to discover who or what he is. But I know he paid Captain Harvey a lot of money for his passage because I saw it change hands.'

'He didn't look very rich. In fact, his clothes were all shabby and torn,' Jan's muffled voice came through the canvas.

'I thought that, too. Now, listen, Jan, what you must do is this. When I give you a signal, which will be to tap five times on the canvas, like this,' Nick hit the canvas with the flat of his hand five times, 'you must make your way to the stern of the boat. Now, it'll be tricky, because even at night there'll be men on watch and the man at the wheel, so you'll have to watch your step. When you get there you'll find I'll have fastened a rope over the stern for you. You must slide down this into the skiff that'll be waiting. Then I can row you and

22

Scarface ashore and no one will be any the wiser. Do you understand?'

'But I thought we were going to Colchester,' Jan complained.

'Wyvenhoe is only about four miles to the east. It won't take you long to walk there. Now, I must go. It'll be tomorrow night. There's no moon, so it couldn't be better. You'll have as long as it takes me to launch the skiff, and get Scarface aboard after I've given you the signal. Right?'

'Right, Nick.'

It seemed an interminable time until Nick gave Jan the signal to move. The Dutch boy had never felt so sick and uncomfortable during the whole voyage as he did during those last hot and airless hours. But at last, quite unmistakably, were five regular blows on the canvas, very near to his head. Cautiously, Jan began to wriggle out of his hiding place.

He allowed a moment to accustom his eyes to the light, because even the moonless night was brighter than the blackness under the canvas, and then began his journey to the stern of the boat, his mouth dry with fear, keeping well into the shadows. He thought the man on starboard watch must have heard his heart beating, although he had his back to him, scanning the marshy coastline, but he made no move to turn round so Jan continued on his way, wriggling past the companionway on his belly, and glad of the noise of voices and laughter coming from below. So far, so good.

But the man at the wheel was another matter. He had his eyes peeled for anything, be it a mudbank or a rat on deck. Getting past him was not going to be so easy. Jan slithered under the great pole stretched the width of the ship where the ropes were held fast and waited a moment for the man at the wheel to turn his head. Then he made a run for it.

'Hey, Boy!' Jan's heart plummeted and he froze where he stood. 'Boy! Is that you, young Nick?'

'Aye, Sir,' Jan muttered, forcing himself to walk towards the man.

'Fetch me a lump o' hard tack, will yer, me guts is gnawin'.'

'Aye, sir.' Jan turned towards the galley and then dropped to his hands and knees and crawled under the shadow of the rail to the stern, up and over the rail and down the rope.

The skiff was already there, waiting.

'Where've you been? We've been here ages,' Nick said, his voice rough with anxiety.

'Never mind that, he's here now, that's the important thing,' Scarface said. 'Quick, lad, into the bottom of the boat. Lie flat so you won't be seen. Right, my boy, pull for the shore.'

Nick pulled on the oars and the boat glided almost silently away from the *Mimosa*, where they could hear the man at the wheel still shouting for his hard tack, towards the saltings that lay just outside the little village of Wyvenhoe.

'If I put you ashore here,' Nick said between pulls, 'you can find your way to Colchester. It's about four miles from the crossroads.'

'I know the area well,' Scarface said. 'I'll see that our young friend doesn't get lost.'

There was a soft bump as the boat grounded. 'Here you are then, mind, the mud is slippery,' Nick warned.

Scarface got out of the boat into the soft, squelchy mud. As Jan made to follow him Nick said softly, 'Come to the quayside at New Hythe tomorrow, Jan. I'll see you there.' Then in a louder voice, 'Give me a push off. That's it. Goodbye.' The skiff glided back to the shadowy bulk of the *Mimosa* and nobody but Nick and Captain Harvey were any the wiser that the boat had lost a passenger, and not even the Captain knew that it had lost two.

Scarface and Jan made their way across the saltings to the village, still sleeping in the dark hours before dawn.

'So, you, too, were anxious to get to England, my young friend,' Scarface said, as they tramped along the empty road. 'From the smell of you, you stowed away in a pretty unsavoury corner, too.' He changed places with Jan. 'I'd prefer it if you kept downwind of me, if you don't mind. When we come to the brook

24

you can wash both yourself and your clothes. They'll soon dry in the warm air.'

'I stowed away in the fleeces,' Jan admitted.

'You *must* have been desperate. I wonder you weren't suffocated.'

'I nearly was.'

'Tell me, why were you so anxious to come to England? Have you relatives in Colchester? I know there's quite a large Dutch community living there now. They came over with the first lot of religious refugees for the most part. Yet you already speak English,' Scarface went on, without giving Jan a chance to answer. 'That in itself is strange.' He gazed at Jan, frowning.

'My mother is English,' Jan explained. 'She went to Holland when she married my father. My father was Dutch, so I speak both languages equally well.'

'Your father *was* Dutch?'

'He died about five years ago.'

'Fighting?'

'No. The coach he and my mother were in overturned. He was killed and my mother was crippled. I've come to England to find her family. It's not safe for her to stay in Holland the way things are there.' He shuddered. 'If she and my sister were to fall into the hands of Alva's men . . .'

Scarface nodded. 'What's her name?'

'Charlotte de Hane.'

'Her English name, I mean.'

'I don't know.'

'Where did she live?'

'I don't know that either. But I've got a picture of the house where she used to live.' Eagerly, Jan felt inside his shirt. But there was nothing there — the picture had gone! It had probably worked out during the repeated wriggling in the tight confines of the fleeces where he had hidden. 'Oh,' he said, horrified, 'it's not there. I must have lost it.'

Scarface patted his shoulder. 'You've come a very long way with very little to go on, lad. England's a big place, you know.

Even if you'd still got your picture I don't think you stand much chance of finding your mother's relatives when you don't even know their name. Did your mother never speak about them?'

'No. There was a terrible row because she wanted to marry my father so she ran away. That's all I know.'

They walked on in silence, each deep in his own thoughts. When they reached the brook Scarface said, 'Jump in, lad. You can't help but come out smelling sweeter.' He smiled and stretched himself on the bank as Jan, gingerly at first and then with increasing enjoyment, splashed and wallowed in the cool, clear running water. When he had had enough he came out and shook himself like a dog.

'Spread your clothes on that bush, yonder, and then come and sit by me till the sun comes up and they dry a little,' Scarface said. 'You can wrap yourself in my cloak.'

Jan did as he was told, then he lay down in the soft grass and was soon asleep. When he woke dawn was breaking, promising a warm, sunny day. Ahead of them lay Colchester, its thatched cottages climbing crazily up the hill from the river. Over to the north lay fields on which stood rows of wooden frames.

'What are those frames?' Jan asked.

'They are called tenter frames,' Scarface explained. 'Colchester is renowned for its cloth industry, Bays and Says for the most part. The cloth is put on those frames to be stretched and dried after it has been fulled at the mill and thickened with teasles.' He stood up. 'Well, come on, my boy. My stomach tells me it's breakfast time. There's a good meal to be had at the Rose and Crown.' He gave Jan a playful cuff, 'And now you look a bit more respectable they'll not deny you entrance.'

Jan walked along beside Scarface, now and then glancing up at him. If it wasn't for the ugly scar he would be quite a handsome man with his thick black hair and fine, regular features. His eyes, too, under their thick black brows were warm and grey and crinkled at the corners when he laughed. But who was

26

he? He had plenty of money — stolen, perhaps? — enough to bribe a passage to England. But what did that say? He could be a pirate or a brigand for all Jan knew. Holland was full of them, plundering and looting their way through the country on the pretext of being on whichever side was winning at the moment.

Jan couldn't understand the terrible fighting that was going on in his country between Catholics and Protestants. It seemed all wrong to him to fight like that. After all, God was God and the Bible that his mother kept carefully hidden said 'Love thy neighbour, do good to them that hate you'. So surely it couldn't be right to murder and torture men just because they worshipped differently. His mother wasn't a Catholic and being English up to now nobody had worried her much. But they lived too close to Amsterdam, with its leanings towards the Catholic Spanish, for comfort, and Jan knew his father would have wanted his family out of the way of any trouble. But his father was dead, so it was up to him, Jan, as man of the house, to organise their escape.

He sighed, a deep, unhappy sigh. A fat lot he'd done so far. True, he'd managed to get himself to England, but his mother and Betkin were still in Holland. And what in the world was he going to do now that he was here? Especially without his picture: his only clue. He frowned, trying to remember what the house in the picture had been like.

Scarface must have read his thoughts. 'I think, Jan de Hane, that the best thing for you is to return to your mother and sister with all possible speed. You're going to do no good in England with such scant information as you've got and your mother is probably sick with worry about you. As soon as I've given you a good breakfast I'll take you to the docks at New Hythe. I'm sure I'll be able to find somebody there who'll give you safe passage back to Amsterdam.'

Jan didn't reply. Miserably he ate the salt beef and pasty Scarface provided and accompanied him to the docks, defeated before he had even begun his search.

27

But in spite of his misery Jan couldn't help a surge of excitement. He was in England, his mother's homeland. The countryside he had walked through with Scarface had been green and peaceful with gentle, undulating fields dotted with thatched cottages but here at New Hythe the docks were busy with ships loading and unloading. There were ropes and barrels of fish, bales of hay and warehouses piled high with wool and cloth. Carts were being pushed and dragged about on their wooden wheels and now and again a carriage drove through, with no regard for anything that might be in its path. It was a bit like Amsterdam, but smaller, with fewer ships on the narrow river and the shouts and cries were in English, a slower, somehow drawling language compared with the sharper guttural Dutch he was used to. The buildings were different, too, not so tall, but the windmills scattered around reminded him of his native land and he felt a pang of home-sickness, even though the last thing he wanted was to be sent back to the Netherlands.

'Wait here, Jan,' Scarface commanded. 'I see the *Golden Sheaf* is in. I'll go and see my good friend Captain Varley. He'll give you safe passage, of that I've no doubt. Don't move from here till I get back.'

Jan watched him board the *Golden Sheaf* and disappear, then he glanced round him. He was in two minds whether to make a run for it. He could hide in one of those warehouses, perhaps make himself a den like he'd had in Amsterdam . . . He began to move towards the nearest door.

But before he had taken many steps a big black and gold coach came rattling over the cobbles. It stopped and a big man with a florid complexion and coarse features heaved himself down the steps.

'Can I hold your horse, sir?' Jan ran forward, eager to earn himself a copper. He knew that he wouldn't last long with no money. The man looked at him blankly, clearly he didn't understand English. Jan repeated the question in Dutch, Scarface had told him there was quite a large Dutch community here in Colchester. This time the man turned and looked him up and down with interest. Then without saying a word he got hold of Jan by the scruff of the neck and bundled him into his coach and lumbered in behind him, banging the door shut.

'Drive on, coachman,' he shouted through the window and Jan was nearly flung to the floor as the coach began to rumble again over the cobbles.

THE PIPE AND JAR

Jan cowered in a corner of the coach. 'Where are you taking me? he asked timidly.

The man smiled at him, revealing teeth that were yellow where they hadn't rotted completely away. 'I'm going to take you home, my boy. You can speak and understand both the Dutch and English tongue?'

Jan nodded. 'My father was Dutch, my mother was — is English, so I was brought up with both languages.'

'Good.' The man nodded, satisfied. 'I think you are just the boy I'm looking for.' He sat back in his seat and folded his hands over his ample stomach. 'But before I take you home I must go to the Bay Hall. You've heard of the Dutch Bay Hall? No? Well, it is the place where all the cloth in Colchester has to be taken to be examined before it can be sold. The Colchester seal of quality is very highly prized, I can tell you. Now, I want you to carry my books for me and keep your eyes and ears open. When we get to my home I shall question you on what you've seen. Remember that.'

With that he lapsed into silence and Jan spent the rest of the journey worrying about disobeying Scarface. Not that he wanted to be shipped straight back to Amsterdam, he'd endured far too much misery and discomfort getting to England to allow himself to be sent straight back from whence he'd come. All the same, he felt he owed Scarface an apology for running off like that. Only he hadn't run off, exactly. You could almost say he'd been kidnapped except that this man seemed quite kind and fatherly, and judging from his fine clothes and smart carriage he was very rich.

The Bay Hall was vast, hot and crowded and the ledgers Jan had to carry for his master were heavy. The babble of voices was incredible and it seemed that neither Dutch nor English understood each other's language for the most part and so tried to make themselves understood to each other by shouting louder. It was quite funny to Jan, understanding both sides, to listen to them talking at cross-purposes, but he said nothing. Keep your eyes and ears open, his master, whose name he discovered was Mynheer Abraham van Migrode, had said, so he did and kept his mouth shut.

He watched carefully as the cloth was examined carefully and then had the Colchester seal clamped to it. These seals fascinated Jan and he tried to get a closer look before someone pushed in front of him. But he'd seen enough, he'd recognise one if he saw it again.

By the time his master was ready to return to his coach Jan was very tired, but he'd made an important discovery.

Abraham van Migrode's house was in a narrow alley off the market place. The road was so narrow and the upper storey overhung so far that it would have been a simple matter to step from his bedroom window to the bedroom of the house opposite. Jan was sent to the kitchen and given beef and pickles and then he was summoned to his master's study. As he went he looked about him. The walls were hung with painted cloths depicting battles at sea and the heavy oak furniture was polished with beeswax until it shone like glass. There was even the fragrance of herbs as he trod the rushes on the floor. Truly, he had been fortunate in coming to the house of such a rich man.

Abraham was sitting at a long table covered in papers, his back to a window that was not just common or garden lattice but was actually glazed. Jan was even more impressed. He smiled at his master.

'What's your name, boy?' Abraham asked.

'Jan de Hane.'

'Where do you come from?'

Better not be too specific. 'Amsterdam.'

'How long have you been in Colchester?'

He had to think about that. Already it seemed like half a lifetime. 'Not very long,' he said.

'How did you get here?' The questions went on and on, just as he had warned Jan they would. But then they changed and Jan found he was no longer being questioned about himself but about the Bay Hall.

'How many cloths were found to be flawed while we were there?'

'Two.'

'What happened to them?'

'They were torn in half and the weavers were fined.'

'Who were the weavers?'

'Jonas de Hest was one and the other was an Englishman, Reuben Scales.'

'What was the fight over?'

'Two English weavers said their families were starving because the Strangers — that's what they seem to call the Dutch people — had stolen their livelihood. The Hall Keeper broke the fight up.'

'What was his name?'

And so it went on, with Jan becoming more and more puzzled. Mynheer van Migrode had been there, he must have seen all these things for himself, so why did he need to ask all these questions?

At last the man sat back in his chair and steepled his fingers. 'Good,' he said, nodding his head. 'You'll do very well for my purpose.'

32

He didn't say what his purpose was and Jan was still puzzled as he lay in the little truckle bed under the eaves that he'd been given. Mynheer van Migrode was clearly a very important man, that much was obvious from the way people had treated him at the Bay Hall, doffing their caps and stammering awkwardly when they spoke to him, so what on earth could he want with him, Jan, a rather shabby little stowaway?

Another thing that worried Jan was Scarface. Scarface had been kind to him and he felt he'd let him down, even though it had been no fault of his own. Perhaps he would be able to send a message to him. Nick would take a message, he felt sure. And that was another thing. Somehow, he must find a way to see Nick at the dockside tomorrow. But he couldn't think about that now. So much had happened since he had smuggled himself aboard the *Mimosa*, yet it was not much more than twenty-four hours ago. His eyelids began to droop.

Then, suddenly, he remembered the most important thing of all. He sat bolt upright in his truckle bed and with trembling fingers undid the leather thong that held his lucky omen. Holding it in his hand he leaned forward to catch the last rays of the dying sun. It was the same! He'd been right! He bounced up and down on his hard little bed in his excitement. It was the same as the seals he'd seen today in the Bay Hall. His lucky omen was nothing less than a Colchester cloth seal. By lucky chance he'd come to the right town to begin his search for his grandfather. And those other letters, too faint to read, probably spelt his grandfather's name, which meant he must be a cloth merchant. All he had to do now was to tramp every street in Colchester until he found the house in his picture. What could be easier?

Happily, he put his head down and immediately fell asleep. But he wouldn't have slept quite so soundly if he'd realised that things weren't going to be quite as easy as he imagined.

The next morning Jan found a new set of clothes laid out to replace his own ragged jerkin and breeches. There was a dark jacket and matching breeches of a softer material than the hard-wearing leather he was used to, and there was also a pair of real shoes. He dressed himself carefully, adjusting the large white collar as well as he could by squinting down at it to make sure it was level.

Abraham van Migrode looked him up and down. 'You'll do,' he said. 'Now, I'm going to send you to work for a good friend of mine. Serve him well and he'll not treat you badly. But, and this is important, what you must do as you go about your work is to keep your eyes and ears open. You will hear things that men only speak about when their tongues have been loosened by drink and they've gone to take coffee to clear their heads. You will hear things that merchants, Dutch and English alike, discuss over a cup of coffee — the latest new-fangled craze — and you will hear of shipping movements, cargoes and more . . . Listen to everything, there are things I'm anxious to know about that only you will be able to find out.'

Jan looked over his shoulder. 'Things to do with the war in Holland?' he asked eagerly.

'Hush, boy.' Abraham looked at him warily. 'What do you know of such things?'

Jan shrugged. 'Not very much. The fighting hadn't reached my village, but I saw Spanish soldiers in Amsterdam and I've heard of the way Alva's men torture and murder. That's why I want to get my mother and sister out of the country.'

'Do as I say and I may be able to help them.' Abraham smiled, showing his rotting teeth. It was a foxy smile and Jan had a moment of misgiving. Should he have trusted this man? Should he have told him so much about his family?

'I have ships trading back and forth to Amsterdam. If you serve me well, my boy, I'll see what can be done for your family.' Abraham patted him on the head as he spoke with such a fatherly gesture that Jan felt immediately ashamed of his suspicions.

A servant took Jan to his new master, Silas Jackson. Silas owned the coffee shop on the corner of the quay at New

34

Hythe. This was a new venture, providing a kind of club for sea captains and merchants, where they could sober up after visiting the ale house or simply enjoy the quieter and more comfortable surroundings than the rowdy and raucous quayside taverns frequented by the crews of the ships in dock. Dutch and English shipmasters alike took advantage of Silas Jackson's coffee house to drink coffee, the latest fashion, and smoke tobacco in long pipes. The coffee was served at tables placed between high-backed settles, these high backs forming little cubicles that provided a certain amount of privacy from eavesdropping neighbours. Much business was done here at the "Pipe and Jar" between merchants of the town and shipmasters. Private business.

Silas Jackson looked Jan up and down. He was a small man with beady eyes and a long nose. 'He ain't very big,' he remarked sourly.

The servant passed him a leather pouch and Jan heard the chink of coins. 'But a likely-enough lookin' lad, for all that,' Jackson added, with more enthusiasm. 'All right, boy, you might as well start work right away. Emily can show you where you'll sleep when we're not so busy. Thass her, over there. She's my daughter.' He jerked his head in the direction of a girl about Jan's own age, with long, dark hair tied back from her face with two bits of rag, busily washing up the small copper mugs that were used to serve the coffee in. 'Here, two jars of coffee and a light to the table over there in the corner, and look lively, boy, we ain't got all night. Emily'll show you how to make the coffee.'

Emily showed him how to grind the brown coffee beans to a powder and make thick treacly liquid with water boiled in a copper urn over the fire. Then she poured it into the little copper mugs with long straight handles. 'Me dad calls these jars,' she explained, 'I dunno why.' She smiled at him, a friendly smile that said it was good to have someone else to share the work and the blows that Silas was not slow to hand out. 'Quick, take them over to that table, I can see me dad watching. Here, you've forgotten the taper.' Emily lit a long spill from the fire and handed it to Jan.

Armed with the coffee jars and the taper Jan made his way to the corner table. '. . . Rode out a storm off the Needles,' one man was saying, 'and then lost the lot to the Sea Beggars.' 'Aye,' said his companion, 'those pirates'll board a ship in a sea like a range o' mountains. Fearless, they are. Many's the time I've gone a hundred miles out of my way to avoid the risk of meeting them.'

'What were you carrying?' a third man asked.

'Spices. Worth a bit, but not as much as what I'll be taking back.' He tapped the side of his nose in a gesture of secrecy. '*The Mermaid*'ll be taking a nice little hoard.' He turned to Jan. 'Bring me some fresh baccy, boy, and a new taper. This lot won't catch.'

He went to do as he'd been bidden and heard of another ship about to leave with a cargo of oysters. 'Not worth a lot but it saves going over empty and the trip back'll make it all worth while,' he heard.

By the end of the day, when the last customers were finishing their pipes and jars and Jan had helped Emily to clear up, his head was reeling with things he had learned from both Dutch and English. He was glad to step out into the cool night air to clear his head.

He'd hardly closed the door behind him when his arm was grabbed.

'Where've you been? I've been hanging about all day waiting for you.' It was Nick's voice that came to him in the darkness.

'Oh!' Jan relaxed. 'You made me jump, grabbing me like that.'

'Where've you been? Have you found your family? By all that's holy, you've got *shoes* on! Where'd you get them? Have you been stealing?' Nick asked, all in one breath.

'No, I haven't been stealing. I've got work. Oh, Nick. I've got so much to tell you. Can we go somewhere so that we can talk?'

'Yes. I'll take you to my place.'

'Do you live near here, then?'

'Yes. This way.' Nick led the way along the quay, past all the paraphernalia of ropes and kegs, chains and barrels of fish that littered the quayside. They dodged a pair of drunken seamen propping each other back to their ship and then slipped between two warehouses. Here there was a flight of steps and at the top Nick pushed open a door hanging on rusty hinges and fastened with rope.

Jan followed him and found himself in a little room made by boarding off a corner of a sail loft with bits of wood carefully nailed together and fixed to the beams.

'Did you do this?' he asked, looking round.

'Yes. I call it my cabin. Look, I even left myself a window so I could look down below. See?' He pointed to a gap in the boards and Jan looked down to the floor below where a great canvas sail was laid out on the floor being patched.

'Do they know you live here?' Jan asked. There was a heap of sacks in the corner, neatly folded to make a bed, and an old table with a stool beside it. Near the door was a hutch with a scrap of bread and a piece of salt pork in it.

'Yes, they don't mind. I've lived here ever since my gran died.' He shrugged. 'Well, they said I'd have to go to the poor house when she died and I didn't want that. I knew I could manage,' he said, with some pride. 'I used to go to school, you know, but then my father was drowned at sea and my mother took sick and died. Gran took me in then but she couldn't afford my schooling so I had to leave. And now she's dead.' He spoke without any hint of self-pity.

Jan looked at him with interest. 'What do you live on?'

'Oh, I get work. Holding horses' heads, running errands and, I told you, sometimes Captain Harvey takes me on.' His eyes sparkled. 'I like that best. One day *I'm* going to be a ship's captain. I'm learning as much as I can about it. Look.' He fished under his sack bed and brought out an old broken telescope. 'I'm learning about the stars with this. You can tell where you are at sea and if you're going in the right direction by the stars, did you know that, Jan?'

'No. I don't know much about things like that,' Jan admitted.

Nick put his most treasured possession back in its place. 'Well, what about you, Jan? What have you been doing? You've got work, you say? Come on, then tell me all about it.'

So Jan told his friend what had happened and how it had all come about because he'd offered to hold a horse's head.

'You're lucky,' Nick said gloomily. 'Nothing like that ever happens to me when I offer to hold anybody's horse. I get a penny if I'm lucky and that's the end of it.'

Jan's face puckered. 'I wish I could have seen Scarface to tell him what I was doing,' he said sadly. 'After all, he was good to me and I wouldn't want him to think I'd simply run off. I hope he'll come to the "Pipe and Jar", then I'll be able to explain to him.'

'If I see him I'll tell him,' Nick said. 'But what do you *do* for this rich Dutchman — what's his name?'

'Mynheer Abraham van Migrode,' Jan said importantly. He dropped his voice. 'I have to keep my eyes and ears open and report what I hear at the "Pipe and Jar"— about shipping movements and cargoes — things like that. It's because I can speak English and Dutch that I'm so useful.'

Nick digested this. 'Do you think he's a spy?' he said at last.

Jan nodded. 'Something like that. And I'll tell you another thing. He said if I did as he asked he might be able to help my mother and sister to get to England.' He looked at Nick triumphantly.

'Whew! That's not bad for only two days in England.'

'And that's not all!' Jan took his medallion from round his neck. 'Do you know what this is?'

'Yes, it's your lucky omen.'

'It's a Colchester seal of quality. They clamp one of these to each piece of cloth to show it's been examined and passed by the Bay Hall. Some of the seals have the name of the clothier on them. I saw them at the Bay Hall when I was there yesterday. They're exactly like this, except,' he rubbed his seal to see if the letters round the edge would come any clearer, 'most of the letters seem to have worn off so you can't read the name on mine.'

The two boys peered at the seal together. 'It looks like a J

38

and there's an L there and is that NGS or NCS at the end?'
Jan said, pointing to each letter in turn.

'I don't know. I'm not very good with letters. I started to
learn to read and write when I was at school but I've forgotten
it all now.' Nick straightened up.

'But you know what this means, don't you?'

'I've told you, I can't . . .'

'No, stupid, I don't mean that. I mean, the fact that my lucky
omen is a Colchester seal means I've come to the right place! My
grandfather must live here, in Colchester, and he's probably a
cloth merchant. I'm sure it's his name written there, if only we
could read what it says. So, all we've got to do now is find his
house.'

'Yes, I see.' Nick's face cleared and he said eagerly, 'Let's have
another look at your picture, then.'

Jan's face fell. 'I can't show it to you. I've lost it. But I can
remember exactly what it was like, can't you?'

'I only saw it once,' Nick said doubtfully.

'Oh, I'm sure you'd recognise it if you saw it,' Jan said, full
of optimism.

The next morning Mynheer Abraham van Migrode came to the
"Pipe and Jar". He chatted jovially with Silas Jackson, using
Jan as interpreter, giving no sign that he recognised the boy.
Presently, he asked for a private room and ordered coffee and
a mutton pie.

'I'll get my daughter to bring it to you right away, Mynheer,'
Silas said with a grovelling smile.

'No, let the boy bring it. I find him easier to converse with,'
Abraham said.

'Quick, then, boy. Jump to it. Fetch the Mynheer what he
asked for.' Ruffled at such an eminent customer Silas gave Jan
a clout that sent him spinning half across the room. 'And don't
forget to ask if he fancy a pipe,' he called after him as he went
through the door.

'Shut the door, boy,' Abraham said. 'Now, tell me quickly, what have you learned?'

Jan recited what he had heard as he had served the customers. Much of it made no sense at all to him and Abraham sometimes made an impatient gesture over what he considered unimportant details. But at the end he said, 'Well done, boy. I shall come again tomorrow. Report to me again then.'

Jan swelled with pride. He was doing important work, he'd gathered that much. He had an idea, though nothing had actually been said, that he was helping to rout the sea beggars, those wild pirates who were the scourge of the sea, who not only attacked ships on the high seas but sailed into coastal ports, sinking fleets at anchor and ransacking the towns. This had happened not long ago in nearby Harwich and people still talked about the devastation there in hushed tones.

For several days Jan was kept busy at the "Pipe and Jar", serving customers with coffee and tobacco, helping Emily to scrub the tables and floors and keeping a sharp ear for information to pass on to his master. He was so busy that he had no time to tramp the streets looking for his house and he became anxious because the days were passing and he was doing nothing to rescue his mother and sister.

Then, one day, as he was scrubbing the front doorstep, Nick came by. 'Oh, Jan,' he said. 'I'm glad I've seen you. I've found your house.'

DANGEROUS WORK

Jan rushed into the bar where Emily was stacking the little coffee jars that helped to give the "Pipe and Jar" its name.

'Where's your father?' he asked.

'Upstairs, having his afternoon snooze. Why? Whatever's the matter, Jan? Is something wrong?' Emily looked at him anxiously.

'No, but I have to go on an urgent message. If your father wakes up . . .'

'If me dad wakes up I'll tell him you've gone to get fresh mutton pies.' She reached into a tin box under the counter. 'Here, take this money. And be sure to bring some back with you.'

'Thanks, Emily.' He grinned at her. She was a good sort; she had a hard life with that father of hers, having to do the work that her mother had done until she rebelled and ran off with a sailor. One day Emily would run off, too, but that was in the future.

'Now, where is my house?' Jan had nearly fallen over Nick in his eagerness to get out of the "Pipe and Jar".

'It's about two miles towards Lexden village, in the street of the Crouched Friars.'

'Come on, then, what are we waiting for?' Jan danced up and down impatiently.

They made their way up the hill from the quay, past the Lepers' Hospital and on to Grub Street. In the distance they could see the ruins of the great Abbey of St John and to their left were the graceful arches of St Botolph's Priory.

'How much further?' Jan said.

'Not much. Past Schergate and Headgate and we're there. Your grandfather must be very rich, Jan.'

'I expect he is. But what make you say that?'

'Because they're all new houses in the street of the Crouched Friars. Ah, here we are. Your grandfather's house is at the other end. I saw them when I came this way to deliver a message to a house in Lexden.'

They walked eagerly on. At last Nick stopped. 'There!' he said. 'That's the house, isn't it?'

Jan stopped too. The house stood a little way back from the road and spanned an archway wide enough for pack ponies to get through to an inner cobbled courtyard. The upper storey was heavily pargeted.

'There you are, see,' Nick said. 'It's got those patterns in the plaster.'

'But my house hadn't got an archway,' Jan said flatly. 'And it was bigger than this one. Much bigger.'

'Oh.' Nick's face fell. 'And I was so sure it was the right one. I recognised it by all that plasterwork because that was what I remembered about the picture you showed me.' He kicked a stone dejectedly. 'But I only saw the picture once.'

They walked back to Nick's cabin, both too disappointed to talk. 'Tell me again exactly what your house was like,' Nick said, flinging himself down on his bed of sacks. 'Then, when I run messages I'll know exactly what I'm looking for.'

'I could draw it for you if I'd got anything to draw on.' Jan looked round the bare little room.

'Draw on the floor.'

'What with?'

'Oh, you haven't got much gumption, have you!' Impatiently, Nick got up and fetched a bucket of water from the corner. 'Dip a stick in that and draw with it. When it dries it'll leave a clean mark on the floor.'

'I haven't got a stick.'

'Well, use your finger then, or a bit of rag.'

Laboriously, Jan did as his friend had suggested, kneeling on the dusty floor and dipping the corner of his jacket in the water.

'There,' he said, when he had finished. 'That's what it looks like. Take a good look and remember it because I don't think it'll last for all that long on the floor.'

'I didn't remember those chimneys,' Nick remarked, with his head on one side.

'The thing to really watch out for is *that*.' Jan pointed to the initials, JCR, set in the plasterwork of the gable.

Nick picked up an old nail and rubbed it bright on his shirt. Then he started to scratch his arm with it.

'Hey, what do you think you're doing?' Jan asked.

'Scratching those letters on my arm so I don't forget their shape. I told you I'm not very good at reading.'

As he watched Nick carefully scratching the surface of his skin Jan felt a surge of feeling towards his friend that he couldn't identify but that brought a funny kind of lump to his throat.

'There,' Nick said, admiring his handiwork. 'I shan't forget what to look for now, shall I?'

Jan got to his feet. 'I must go back. Emily said she'd look after things till I got back but her father will be awake by now and . . . oh, crumbs, I've forgotten the mutton pies!'

It was Saturday night. The "Pipe and Jar" was full to overflowing and the atmosphere was so thick with smoke that you couldn't see from one end of the coffee house to the other. Jan was kept busy, running between tables, carrying coffee and clearing the empty jars away. Some of the customers were getting to know the lively little lad who could converse equally well with both Dutch and English customers and he was often slipped a ha'penny for his pains, which he carefully hoarded in the straw pallet in the corner of Silas's room where he slept.

'Bring me a jar, lad, and look lively.' Jan thought he recognised the voice, but as he glanced round the only person he recognised was Sir John Dalrymple, the local magistrate, a big man with a face like a boiled lobster, who Silas usually served himself, fawning over him till Jan felt sick. 'Here, boy, over here.' A youngish, dark-haired man sitting with the magistrate snapped his fingers. 'And bring one for Sir John too.'

'Right away, sir.' Jan hurried to fetch the coffee. He realised now that the stranger had a voice a little like Scarface's, but he didn't look at all like him. This man was cleanshaven and had no disfiguring scar.

'Thanks, boy.' The stranger tossed Jan a penny without looking up.

For the rest of the evening Jan's thoughts kept turning towards Scarface. He'd never clapped eyes on him since the day, nearly three weeks ago, that he'd arrived in England. In fact, he hadn't even thought of him much. Nick hadn't seen him either, so neither of them had had the chance to explain Jan's disappearance that day at the docks.

Jan often saw Nick. His little cabin in the sail loft was only a few hundred yards from the "Pipe and Jar" so it was an easy matter for Jan to slip round there when business was slack, or when Silas was having his nap — as long as he didn't forget to bring back the mutton pies. His backside still smarted when he remembered the consequences of that fateful afternoon.

The two boys would sit in Nick's cabin together and Jan would tell his friend the more interesting snippets of information he'd gleaned, like the news, earlier in the week, that a cargo of rubies was due in from an Eastern state, travelling in a ship disguised as

44

an old fishing vessel to 'fox those pirates, the Dutch Sea Beggars' Jan had explained.

It was often late when the last customer left. One night Jan was just barring the door when a shadowy figure appeared. It was Nick. 'I've got to speak to you. Something important,' he whispered.

'I'll come and see you tomorrow,' Jan whispered back, looking over his shoulder to where Emily was mopping up the last table while Silas counted the night's takings, yawning loudly. Silas never ever drank the coffee he served, he said it kept him awake at night.

'No, it's *important*. Come tonight,' Nick hissed.

Jan hesitated. Perhaps Nick had found his grandfather's house. The right one. 'Look,' he said, 'I'll have to go to bed. I sleep in the landlord's room so I'll have to wait till he's asleep, but then I'll sneak out and come to your cabin.'

'All right. But try not to be too long.' Nick disappeared into the darkness.

'What you doin', boy? Thass takin' you some time to bar the door,' Silas growled.

'The bolt jammed. There, that's better.' Jan rammed the bolt home and turned away to follow him up the stairs.

It wasn't long before Silas was snoring heavily. Silently, Jan crept out of the room and down the stairs, careful to avoid the one that creaked. Then across the room with its high settles making dark shadowy corners and over to the door. He held his breath as he drew the bolt back, slowly so as to make no noise, and slipped out into the cool night air. It smelled of sea and mud, tar and wool, all mingled together, but it was fresh after the stale, tobacco-laden air of the "Pipe and Jar" and Jan took great gulps as he hurried along the deserted quay.

'I thought you were never coming,' Nick said impatiently when Jan reached the cabin. 'You've been *hours*.'

'I had to wait till I was sure he was asleep,' Jan spoke irritably. He was tired, he'd had a long day and he wanted to go to bed. If it hadn't been that he was so anxious for news of his family he'd have made Nick wait till tomorrow. 'Well, what have you got to tell me?'

'I've seen Scarface!' Nick said triumphantly.

'Oh, is that all. I'd have thought you could have waited till tomorrow to tell me that.' Jan yawned. 'When did you see him?'

'Earlier this evening. He told me he'd just come off the *Golden Sheaf*. I told him about you and what you were doing.'

'Oh, you shouldn't have told him. I told you you weren't to tell anybody. You could get me into terrible trouble.'

Nick shifted uncomfortably. 'We can trust Scarface.'

'How do you know that? We don't know anything about him. He could be an enemy agent.'

'*I* think we can trust him. Captain Harvey wouldn't give passage to a traitor.'

'He would if he didn't know. Anyway, he was paid well. Some people will do anything for money.' Jan was furious and he showed it. 'Anyway, what did Scarface say?' he asked in a more reasonable tone.

'He asked me if I'd seen you. He said he'd arranged your passage back to Amsterdam — and paid for it — but when he came ashore again you'd gone. He wasn't pleased about that, I can tell you.'

'Did you explain?'

'Yes. I told him you'd been practically kidnapped and that you hadn't had time to leave a message or anything.'

'Is that all you told him?' Jan asked, beginning to look relieved.

'Well, no. Naturally enough he wanted to know a bit more so I told him about Mynheer van Migrode getting you work in the "Pipe and Jar".' Nick looked at Jan out of the corner of his eye. 'Scarface says Mynheer van Migrode is not to be trusted,' he added, wriggling uncomfortably.

'Rubbish,' Jan said. He glared at Nick. 'I hope you didn't tell him any of the things I've told you.'

Nick hung his head. 'I told him about the ship with the rubies in it,' he admitted. 'Well, it's a good story and I expect it's reached harbour safely by now.'

'You told him that! A fine friend you've turned out to be,' Jan said bitterly. 'And this is what you've dragged me here in the middle of the night to tell me? That you've told this stranger all the secrets I trusted you with?'

'No.' Nick shook his head and his tone was serious. 'That's not all. The important thing is that Scarface said I was to warn you to be careful. He says you are doing very dangerous work, work that if you put a foot wrong could cost you your life. And that you're working for the *wrong side*!'

Jan digested this. After his first momentary misgivings about Mynheer van Migrode he had never doubted his fatherly employer's good intentions. He always treated Jan kindly and with encouragement. And hadn't he promised — a promise he'd repeated several times — to help bring Jan's mother and Betkin to England and safety?

'I don't believe it,' he said at last. 'I don't know what Scarface's game is but I don't trust him. Do you remember when we asked him what he did for a living? He never actually told us, did he?'

'What, over in Amsterdam, you mean? He didn't get the chance, did he? Those men with knives came in. And they looked like Spaniards to me.'

'You're making that up. You can't remember what they looked like.' Jan stood up. 'I'm going back to the "Pipe and Jar". I'm disappointed in you, Nick.'

'Wait a minute. Scarface said you'd be doing a great service if you passed what you learned at the "Pipe and Jar" to him. But you mustn't speak to him. You must tell me and I'll pass the message on.'

'Well, the first message you can pass on is to tell him to go and jump,' Jan said, rudely. 'And don't think I shall ever tell you anything again, because I shan't.'

But as he made his way back to the "Pipe and Jar" Jan looked over his shoulder several times. A boy trussed up and thrown in the water on the ebb tide would hardly make a splash and would quickly be carried down river and out to sea.

A week later, serving coffee at the "Pipe and Jar", Jan learned that the ruby-laden ship, in spite of being disguised as an old fishing boat to fox the Sea Beggars, had been raided, her cargo removed and the crew left with their throats slit.

THE OLD WAREHOUSE

At the earliest opportunity Jan went to find Nick and tell him this news. But his friend wasn't in his cabin and enquiries on the dockside, where everyone knew Nick's cheerful, cheeky face, yielded the information that he'd gone on a trip with Captain Harvey and probably wouldn't be back before the week was out.

At least, Jan consoled himself, that meant that Nick wouldn't be able to pass any further information to the traitor, Scarface.

He wandered to the end of the quay where it was quiet. Nobody much came up this end, all the activity was confined to the end nearest the town where the new warehouses were. Here the buildings were all derelict and decaying. He sat down on a bollard near to an old warehouse that jutted out over the water. In days gone by ships could have moored underneath and had their cargo dropped straight down into the hold from trapdoors in the floor. But ships were bigger now and the old building was no longer used.

Jan threw a pebble into the black water of the high tide. It was too much of a coincidence to imagine that Scarface had had nothing to do with the raiding of the boat carrying the rubies. It had been disguised in such a way that the piratical Sea Beggars wouldn't have looked twice, so it was surely nothing to do with them. And it was not the sort of information his master, Mynheer van Migrode, was interested in, although he noted it down, like he did everything Jan told him.

He went to the edge of the quay and stood gazing downriver in the gathering darkness. Perhaps this would teach Nick a lesson and he would realise that Scarface was not to be trusted. He had to admit that he missed his friend and was unhappy that they had parted on such bad terms. But there was no sign of Captain Harvey's *Mimosa* coming up river on the tide; there was only the vague shadow of a boat anchored slightly downriver of the quay, in mid-channel. It was a strange place for a boat to anchor, he thought, absent-mindedly, but he couldn't recognise it in the gloom. He turned to go back to the "Pipe and Jar". Silas would be shouting for him and he knew he was due for a good cuff for being away at the busiest time and leaving Emily to cope.

But then he stopped in his tracks. He thought he heard a cry. It sounded like a muffled shout and it came from the direction of the old warehouse.

With his heart in his mouth he crept nearer in the shadows to see if he could see where it came from. It seemed to be coming from inside the warehouse.

'Keep his head covered.' He heard the words quite plainly, spoken in Dutch. And then, 'Now, down you go, my fine friend, back to where you'll get what you deserve.'

There was a creaking noise and then a splash and then the steady pull of muffled oars and Jan could just make out the shadowy form of a skiff moving towards the anchored boat.

What was all that about, he wondered? Had those men come from the boat in the river to bring someone ashore? No, '*down you go,*' they'd said and then there had been a splash. Almost fearful of what he might see there, Jan peered down into the murky waters of the Colne. But there was nothing disturbing its oily calm apart from the usual scum and litter of rotting vegetation. Jan felt confused. What could have happened?

He stepped back into the shadows as he heard the faint sound of oars again. The skiff was coming back! He froze against the wall of the warehouse and waited. After a few minutes he heard the boat bump against the quay. He edged nearer. It sounded as if the men were pulling the boat up into the warehouse through the trapdoor. He peered through a chink in the rotting wooden side of the building, his palms sweating. There were two men, as far as he could see in the darkness, and they appeared to be wearing long black cloaks that enveloped them from head to foot. When they were satisfied that the boat was safe they slipped out and away over the fields, ghostly figures that merged into the black night.

With a shudder, Jan hurried back to the "Pipe and Jar", where even Silas Jackson's strong hand boxing his ears had a comforting feel.

Jan waited impatiently for Nick's return. Every day he went to his friend's cabin, sure that when Nick heard about the ruby boat he would admit that he'd been wrong about Scarface. And there was also the business of the warehouse to tell him about.

While he waited he listened to the conversations that took place in the "Pipe and Jar", a good deal of it about the war in Holland which he couldn't understand but he passed what he heard to his grateful master to sift and make of it what he might.

'You are doing valuable work, my boy,' Abraham said, patting him on the head. 'It will all help to bring the war in Holland to a swifter end so that our people taking refuge in this country can return in safety. Oh, no, I haven't forgotten your mother,' seeing Jan's look of anxiety. 'Never fear, my boy. Now, which boat did you say . . .? And how many men will be on it?'

'The *Marigold*. It sails on Thursday.'

The men they spoke of were armed Dutchmen, gathered from families in the town ready and eager to go back to fight for the Prince of Orange against Alva's tyranny.

'Speak of this to no one,' Abraham warned. 'The fewer people who know the boat is leaving the better. But,' he patted Jan on the head, 'I know you are the soul of discretion, my boy.' He smiled at him and a drop of gravy from his mutton pie dribbled down his chin.

At last Nick came back. Jan was in his cabin waiting for him with two pasties and some weak ale.

'I thought you'd *never* come back,' Jan said. 'I've got such a lot to tell you I don't know where to begin.'

'The beginning's as good a place as any,' Nick said, tucking into his pasty with obvious relish. He was relieved that Jan was no longer angry with him. He liked his Dutch friend and valued his friendship highly.

So Jan told him about the ruby boat being raided. 'You see,' he finished, cramming the last of his pasty into his mouth. 'I was right. Scarface *is* a traitor. He must have got news to the Sea Beggars to raid that old fishing boat.'

'How do you know it was the Sea Beggars?' Nick argued.

'What? All the crew left with their throats slit? Who else but those barbarians would do such a thing?'

Nick was not convinced. 'I can't see Scarface being in league with the Sea Beggars,' he said. 'He doesn't look like a pirate. He's too much of a . . .' he peered down into his empty beer mug, searching for the right word, '. . . gentleman.'

'Bah!' Jan finished his ale and wiped his mouth on his sleeve. 'Look at his face. With that scar he looks *exactly* like a pirate!'

'Maybe you're right,' Nick agreed doubtfully.

'Well, I think you'd better not pass any more messages on to him for the time being,' Jan advised. 'Just to be on the safe side.'

'No, all right.' Nick still sounded doubtful. 'But what shall I say to him?'

'Don't say anything. Just keep out of his way.'

'I'll think about it.' Nick refused to commit himself. He was quiet for a few minutes. Then, 'Is that all you've got to tell me?'

'No, it isn't. A very odd thing happened only the other night. I was up by the old warehouse at the end of the quay looking

52

to see if your boat was in sight when I saw, or rather heard, something very strange.'

Jan told Nick about the shadowy figures and the boat anchored in the river.

'What sort of boat was it?' Nick asked when he had finished.

'I couldn't see. It was too dark. But it was a funny shape and had an enormous bowsprit.'

'Did you hear what they said?'

'Yes, they spoke in Dutch and they must have had somebody with them because they said, "Down you go, my fine friend, back to where you'll get what you deserve." Or something like that.'

'Down you go where? What did they do, chuck him in the water?'

'I don't know. I couldn't see anything in the water, yet I'm sure I heard a splash.'

Nick wriggled impatiently. 'What then?'

'They rowed out to the big boat and then came back and left the skiff in the warehouse. That's all.'

'Perhaps they kidnapped him.'

'Who?'

'The man you said they had with them. Perhaps they tied him up and took him to the big boat and left him there.'

Jan shook his head and sighed. 'I just don't know what to think.'

Nick stood up. 'When did this happen?'

'A couple of days ago.'

'Let's go and see if it's still there.'

'What, now?'

'Yes. It's getting dark so no one'll see us.'

'All right.' Jan followed Nick out of the cabin and down the rickety staircase and along the quay to where the old warehouse stood, shrouded in shadows, jutting out over the water.

They stepped inside. It had a dank, musty smell, a mixture of river smells and long-forgotten cargoes that had been stored there. It was full of eerie shadows.

'I can't see the boat,' Jan whispered. 'They must have come and taken it away.'

'What's that, down by your foot?' Nick said, also keeping his voice to a whisper.

Jan bent down. 'It's a book. Looks like a Bible. I wonder where it came from.' He slipped it inside his shirt. 'Mind where you put your feet,' he said, still whispering, 'some of these floorboards look quite rotten.'

Nick walked carefully across the floor. 'They're quite rotten here,' he said in his normal voice as he became braver. 'Look, there's a hole. You can see the river underneath.'

'And if you wander about in places like this that's very likely where you'll end up. In the river.' A voice said from high above them.

They both froze. Then slowly they raised their heads and looked up. There, in the dim evening light, looking down at them from the wooden gallery that ran the length of the warehouse, was Scarface.

Instinctively, both boys turned to run, but Scarface took a leap from the gallery and barred their way. They could see the glint of a pistol at his belt and he was clad from head to foot in black.

'What do you think you're doing here?' he hissed.

'Jan saw some funny . . .' Nick began, but Jan clamped his hand over his mouth.

'Don't tell him. Don't tell him *anything*. Remember the ruby boat.'

Scarface looked from one boy to the other and back again. Then he sighed. 'You've no idea, have you? You've absolutely no idea what filthy work you've got yourselves mixed up in. You don't know who you're working for, nor who to believe. Why don't you keep right out of it all? It's man's work and not fit for youngsters like you to even know about, let alone get mixed up in.' He stepped towards them. 'But if you must get mixed up in it for God's sake why can't you use your cunning to aid the right side! Now, be off with you, and don't let me

54

see you anywhere near this place again or I'll have you taken before the magistrate.' He gave them a push towards the door. 'Work that's done here is not for your young eyes. Go, quickly, or you could end up hanging upside down with your head in the water.'

There was no doubt he meant what he said. The two boys backed away from him and didn't stop running until they reached Nick's cabin. Once inside they barred the door.

'What do you think Scarface was doing there?' Nick said in a low voice, afraid that even here, in the safety of his cabin, they might be overheard. 'Do you think he was waiting for someone?'

'It seemed like it,' Jan agreed. 'Perhaps he was waiting for those men I saw the other night. Perhaps he *was* one of the men I saw the other night.'

'But I thought you said they were Dutch.'

'Oh, yes, so I did.' Jan pulled the book he'd picked up in the warehouse from where he'd hidden it in his shirt. 'Look, this is a Bible, just as I thought. And it's a Dutch one.'

'Perhaps that's what Scarface came to look for. Perhaps Scarface and his friends had kidnapped somebody and drowned them in the river.' Nick warmed to his tale. 'And Scarface had come back to make sure all traces had been removed.'

Jan nodded. 'And that's why he warned us off, because he was afraid we might stumble on something.' Jan held up the Bible. 'Like this. You see, I told you he wasn't to be trusted.'

CLUES AND NEWS

When Jan got back to the "Pipe and Jar" Emily was in the kitchen making mutton pies. Silas had discovered that it was cheaper for Emily to make the pies and pasties than for him to buy them in from the pastry cook so that was another duty added to her already heavy burden of chores.

'You'd better get into the coffee house,' she warned, brushing her hair out of her eyes with a floury hand. 'Me dad's shouting for you.' She looked over her shoulder anxiously. 'I covered up for you as best I could, Jan, but you've been gone an awful long time.'

'Yes, I know. I'm sorry, Emily.' He smiled at her. Poor Emily, she had a hard life with that father of hers; he treated her worse than a servant and hardly ever gave her so much as a kind word.

He hurried into the coffee house. There were not many people in at this hour and although Silas would always pretend to be overworked there was little to do.

'Where you bin, you varmit? You're ollwus runnin' off these days. I don't pay you to idle your time away watchin' the boats,

56

you're here to work.' Silas gave him a box on the ears that sent him reeling. 'Now, git them tables cleared. An' take that man in the corner a light. You'll be out on your ear if you don't look slippy.'

Jan knew better than to argue with Silas, although it was an empty threat he'd made and well Jan knew it. While Mynheer van Migrode passed a bag of coins over each week it was more than Silas dare do to sack his little pot boy. At the same time, Jan was not a boy to invite beatings so he kept on the right side of the landlord of the "Pipe and Jar" as far as he could.

He hurried over to the man in the corner; he was the only customer at the moment. Jan had often seen him in the coffee house, drinking his coffee and smoking his pipe, a shabby, middle-aged Dutchman, who seemed to have no friends and few acquaintances. He grunted as Jan handed him a taper.

'Anything else I can get you, sir?' Jan asked.

'Only an end to this damned war,' the man replied sullenly, turning back to his coffee.

Jan cleared the other tables and took the jars down to the kitchen.

'I'll wash these, Emily,' he said, seeing her expression as he carried them in. 'Don't worry.'

Emily raked a batch of pies out of the oven and put another lot in. Then she came over to where Jan was dipping the little copper jars into hot water and putting them to drain.

'Is that fat Dutchman who comes in sometimes your uncle?' she asked, picking up a cloth and beginning to dry them.

'Oh, no,' Jan answered. He thought carefully for a moment. 'He just . . . befriended me.'

'Oh, I see.' Emily dried a few more jars. 'Haven't you got any family?'

'I've got a mother, over in Holland. My father's dead.'

'What are you doing over here, then?'

'Looking for my grandfather.' Seeing Emily's puzzled look, he explained. 'My mother is English. She married my father, who was a Dutch sea captain. He's dead now and my mother

57

is crippled so she can't walk. I've come to find my grandfather
to see if he'll pay to bring her to England because of the dreadful
things that are happening in Holland.'

Emily nodded. 'Yes, I've heard about the terrible war over
there. They often talk about it in the coffee house, don't they?'
She frowned. 'Why didn't your mother write and ask your
grandfather to send her the money? There's always someone
on one of the ships coming over who'll carry a message.'

Jan shook his head. 'It's not as easy as that. You see, my mother
ran away to marry my father. Her father didn't want her to marry
him and there was a fearful row. My mother doesn't even know
I've come to England. She'd never have agreed to let me come
if she'd known.'

'Where does your grandfather live?'

'That's just it, I don't know. My mother never spoke of him.
But I think it must be somewhere near Colchester, in a big house.
I had a picture of it once, but I lost it.'

'What's his name?'

'I don't know that either.'

Emily looked at him, her blue eyes full of sympathy. 'You
haven't got much to go on, have you? Why don't you ask Sir
John Dalrymple? He's often in here and he knows just about
everybody, being the local magistrate.'

'I might,' Jan said. But he didn't suppose he would. He didn't
think he'd have the courage to talk to such an important man.

They finished washing the little coffee jars and Emily gave
him a pie to eat, made from left-over pastry. 'I had a friend
once,' she said thoughtfully, watching as he munched. 'She
worked as a scullery maid at a place where one of the rooms
was always kept locked up. Nobody was ever allowed in it,
except, of course, once a month when one of the servants went
in to dust it.'

'Oh, yes,' Jan said, without much interest.

She helped herself to a crust of bread. 'Sal said she went in
there, once.'

'Oh, yes.'

'It had a bed in it with silk hangings. And there were silk hangings on the walls. Sal said she thought it had been the man's daughter's room. And when she went away he ordered it to be kept just the way it had always been. Even the herbs in the pots round the room were to be kept the same.'

Jan looked up. 'Where did she go? The daughter, I mean.'

'Dunno. Sal didn't know either. Just that she went away. Apart from the room being always kept the same nobody ever talked about it. I expect she ran away. That's what I'm going to do when I've got enough money.'

Jan stood up and brushed the crumbs off his chin. 'Where is this house?' he asked. He didn't blame Emily for wanting to run away from the "Pipe and Jar" and her horrible father.

'Oh, a good distance. It's out Boxted way, I think. I've never seen it, but Sal used to tell me it was quite grand.' She shrugged. 'I don't know how grand. She might have made it all up for all I know.'

'I might go and take a look when I get a chance,' Jan said casually. It wouldn't do to build too much on what might only be the fanciful imaginings of a scullery maid.

'Boy! What you doin' down there in that kitchen? Thass takin' you some time to wash them jars, ain't it!' Silas's voice came thundering from the coffee house. 'Come you up here and see to the customers. We got a shop full of people and nobody but me to see arter 'em.'

Jan and Emily exchanged glances. 'You'd better go,' Emily said, making a face. 'And take the tray with you so he'll see you've been working.'

Jan grinned at her as he picked up the tray. He liked Emily.

Silas's 'shop full of customers' was two men, one of whom had joined the man in the corner, and the other sitting alone some distance from the other two. Jan was surprised to see anybody talking to the usually solitary Dutchman and he took his time clearing the table in the next alcove to see what he could pick up from the conversation.

'. . . be all over the town before the week's out,' the newcomer

59

said. 'Come Sunday people'll want to know where the Predikant is.'

'Three days you say he's been missing?' the solitary man asked.

'Yes, and from the look of his house he went in a hurry.' The newcomer dropped his voice so that Jan had to strain to catch his words. 'And he didn't go willingly, either.'

Jan was forced to move on or he would have attracted suspicion. Later, as the coffee house filled up, he listened for more news. He knew that by the word Predikant they had referred to the Minister of the Dutch Church here in Colchester — that was what he was always called. If he'd heard right and if what the two men were discussing was true, that meant that Mynheer Verlender, the Dutch Minister, was missing, taken from his home by force. Jan had often seen Mynheer Verlender about his business in the town; he seemed a quiet, inoffensive sort of man.

But although he listened carefully, strangely enough, not another word was said on the subject in the coffee house all evening.

Nevertheless, Jan knew that it must be true. Because he'd seen — or almost seen — it happen! He only wished he'd been able to see what they had done with the poor man. But at least he'd got Mynheer Verlender's Bible upstairs, hidden under his straw pallet. That was proof enough.

This news was far too important to wait for a visit from Mynheer van Migrode. Mynheer had paid him a visit yesterday so it was unlikely that he would come again for a few days. Sometimes he didn't come for over a week when he had to go on one of his business trips. Jan knew that somehow he must find an opportunity to go to Mynheer van Migrode's house in Angel Lane and tell him what he knew. And without delay.

He managed to slip out early the next morning whilst Silas was out on board a ship just in from Arabia bargaining over a fresh supply of coffee beans.

First he went to find Nick. His friend was still asleep, curled up on his bed of sacks. He sat up and knuckled his eyes as Jan burst in.

'Wassa time?' he grumbled, still only half awake.

'Time you were awake and out of bed,' Jan said, giving him a good shake. 'Listen, I've got things to tell you.'

'Oh, no,' Nick groaned. 'I can't stand it. What is it now?' He got up and staggered over to the corner where he kept his bucket of water and dipped his head in it. Then he picked up his cup and scooped out a cupful and drank it.

'Ugh, you are filthy,' Jan said, making a face. 'You should have had a drink before you dunked your head, not after.'

'Should I? Yes, I s'pose I should.' Nick grinned. 'I usually have a drink *while* I'm dunking my head, to tell you the truth.'

'You're disgusting,' Jan said. But he grinned at his friend as he spoke.

'Well?' Nick shook his head, spraying water everywhere. 'I'm awake now. What are these things you've got to tell me?'

'First of all, I was talking to Emily yesterday. She told me she used to have a friend who worked as a scullery maid for a man who kept a room shut up in his house.'

'Why did he do that?'

'Don't interrupt and I'll tell you. His daughter had gone away and he said the room was never to be changed.'

Nick wasn't impressed. 'What about it, then?'

'It might have been my mother,' Jan said feebly.

'It might have been a fairy story, too. You know how girls like to make things up. I reckon it's a lot of rubbish, myself.'

Jan's face fell. He'd hoped Nick would offer to go and investigate for him.

'Where is this house, anyway?' Nick asked.

'Over Boxted way.'

'Boxted! Good grief, that's miles away.'

'Don't you sometimes have to take messages over in that direction?'

'Now and again.' Nick nodded reluctantly.

'Well, if you do . . . All I'm asking is that you keep your eye open for the house.'

'I *always* keep my eye open for your house, wherever I go. Look!' Nick thrust his arm under Jan's nose. 'It's still there, where I scratched the letters.'

'Yes, I know. It's just . . . well, keep a special eye open when you're over Boxted way.' Jan was a bit crestfallen, he'd hoped Nick would have been just a little excited.

'Is that all you woke me up to tell me?' Nick still wasn't very good tempered.

'Yes,' Jan said sullenly, going to the door. Then he spun round. 'No, there is something else. I heard in the coffee house last night that Mynheer Verlender is missing. He's been gone for three days.'

'Who's Mynheer Verlender?'

'The Minister at the Dutch Church. You must have seen him about the town. A tall, thin man, always carries a Bible.'

'Always carries a *Bible*!' Nick's eyes widened. 'And you think . . .'

Jan took the Bible out of his shirt. 'Yes, I think this is Mynheer Verlender's Bible. And I think I know what happened to him because I saw — or nearly saw — it happen. I'm going to Mynheer van Migrode's house now, to tell him.'

'But I thought he said you weren't to go to his house, he'd come to you.'

'I know. But this is important and he might not come to the "Pipe and Jar" for several days.'

Nick nodded. 'I suppose you had better go and tell him, then.'

Jan hurried to the house in Angel Lane where Abraham van Migrode lived. The market place was already thronged with people seeking the freshest vegetables and he had to dodge between the crowds to reach the narrow street.

A servant answered his knock.

'I must see Mynheer van Migrode. It's very important,' Jan said.

The servant looked him up and down. There was something

62

about the scruffy little urchin that he recognised. Perhaps it was the clothes. Even though they were stained with coffee now and none too clean he remembered being sent to buy them from the old clothes woman not many weeks ago. So this must be the boy who the master had brought home with him and who'd stayed the night.

'You'd better wait here,' he said grudgingly. 'I'll see if the master will see you.'

'It's very important,' Jan insisted. 'It's about . . .'

'Wait here.'

The servant left him in the passage, which was like a dark tunnel with doors opening off it but no windows to lighten it, and went to knock on a door at the end. Jan clutched the Bible to him under his shirt and waited, his heart thumping.

The door opened and he heard the murmur of voices and then Mynheer's voice shrill with fury. 'Send him away. I told you I was not to be disturbed under *any* circumstances. Send him away. At once!'

The servant murmured something else.

'I *told* him he was never to come here. Get him out of the house by the back way. But get him out. *And quick!*'

There was a murmur of voices and this time a third voice joined in. 'Do as your master bids you, my fine friend.'

Suddenly, Jan's blood ran cold. He remembered hearing that voice before.

He didn't wait to be put out of the house by the back door; with fumbling fingers he let himself out the way he'd come in and he didn't stop running till he reached the refuge of Nick's cabin.

THE HOUSE

Nick was splicing a rope for his boat, sitting in the middle of the floor. Captain Harvey had given him an old dinghy and Nick, not content with oars, had rigged himself a lugsail for it. He found his little boat another useful source of income because he could use it to collect cockles from the mud at low tide, or to catch the odd flounder, and it was surprising how much flotsam and jetsam he managed to find and make a few pence on. His boat was a fairly recent acquisition and one of which he was particularly proud.

He looked up when Jan burst in.

'By all that's holy!' was all he could find to say when Jan had finished telling him. 'Are you sure?'

'Absolutely.' Jan nodded emphatically. 'I heard him say, "Do as your master bids you, my fine friend." And it was "my fine friend" that made me so sure, because that's what I heard that night in the old warehouse. "Down you go, my fine friend," I heard. And it was the *same voice*, I'm sure of it.'

Nick stopped his splicing. 'But what would the same man be

64

doing kidnapping the Dutch Minister *and* talking to Mynheer van Migrode?'

'I don't know. I don't know at all.' Jan shook his head.

'They must be on the same side,' Nick said after a while. 'But I don't understand . . .'

Jan gave a deep sigh. 'No, Nick, I don't understand either. I don't understand anything any more.'

The two boys looked at each other. They no longer knew who or what to believe.

Just as Scarface had predicted.

Jan went back to the coffee house. On his way he passed a very smartly dressed man with a cutlass hanging from his belt. Jan looked at him. Only naval men wore cutlasses instead of swords and Jan didn't know any naval men, yet there was something very familiar about this man. Jan frowned. He couldn't think where he could have seen him before. As they drew level the man looked straight at him and Jan could have sworn he winked. More puzzled than ever Jan went on his way.

But all thoughts of the strange man were soon put out of his head. The coffee house was buzzing with the news that the *Marigold*, with its shipload of Dutch refugees recruited from the town to go back and fight for the Prince of Orange against the Duke of Alva, had narrowly escaped being sunk off Languard Point. All hands had been rescued and the men were now making their way as best they might, on foot for the most part, back to Colchester from Harwich.

A week later Mynheer van Migrode came to the coffee house for his usual jar of coffee and mutton pie, served to him in the cosy privacy of a private room reserved for those who preferred to smoke in quiet solitude. As was the custom, Jan served him, taking his jar and tobacco on a tray and then coming back with the taper.

'Well, my boy?' Mynheer van Migrode appeared not to notice the boy's hand trembling as he held the taper for him to light his pipe. 'And what news have you for me?' He smiled at Jan, his teeth more yellow and rotten than ever and Jan felt a sudden cold shiver down his spine. He licked his lips. 'The *Marigold*, sir. She had to put in to Harwich after being attacked off the Languard Point. The men are making their way back to the town as best they may on foot.'

Mynheer van Migrode nodded and made a note of this. 'Anything more?'

'The *Vanguard* came in with a cargo of woad for dyeing, and the *Grace* has taken cloth to London, but that's common knowledge, sir.'

'It is, indeed.' Nevertheless, Mynheer van Migrode put it down in his book.

Jan watched him warily. He had made no reference to Jan's untimely visit to his house the other morning, but it might arouse his suspicions if Jan had no vitally important news to give him and he might wonder what the reason was for his sudden appearance.

'No doubt by this time you've heard that Mynheer Verlender is missing,' he said.

'Yes.' Mynheer van Migrode drew on his pipe. 'Sad, that. Very sad. No one seems to know what's happened to him.' He shot a swift glance at Jan. 'You've heard nothing, boy? No hint of where he might have gone?'

'No, sir.' It was the first time that Jan had lied to his master.

Mynheer van Migrode slurped his coffee, drew on his pipe and wolfed his mutton pie in turn. Jan watched him and suddenly a thought dawned on him, a thought that had been lurking in his mind for some time without actually forming itself into words. He didn't like Mynheer Abraham van Migrode. Apart from the fact that he was fat, ugly and greedy there was something — Jan searched for the right word — something sinister about him that made the flesh creep and sent cold shivers down the spine.

'Now, boy,' Mynheer van Migrode wiped his mouth with the back of his hand, 'I want you to do something for me.'

'Yes, sir.' Jan looked at him doubtfully.

'I want you to take a message for me to the landlord of the "Woolpack" out on the Donyland Road. I'll make it all right with Jackson, here. I'll tell him I need you for the rest of the day. It's a tidy step to the "Woolpack".'

'Yes, sir.'

'Now, what I want you to say is this — "Make ready for the hunting party. Tonight they're after the wild boar".' Mynheer van Migrode smiled his yellow smile. 'Say it after me.'

'Make ready for the hunting party. Tonight they're after the wild boar.'

'Good boy.' Mynheer van Migrode patted him on the head and somehow his gesture was no longer fatherly but somehow menacing.

Silas was reluctant to let him go for the rest of the day but a gold coin made the parting easier.

Jan immediately went to Nick's cabin.

Nick had just come in and was lying stretched out on his bed. He looked up when Jan entered. 'I'm exhausted,' he said. 'Look at my poor feet, covered in blisters.' He held his feet up in the air for Jan to see.

'Covered in dirt, you mean. I can't see any blisters. Your feet are as hard as horses' hooves, they'd never blister. Why, what have you been doing?'

'I had to run an errand out Mile End way and I thought, having got a lift in a tinker's cart most of the way, that I'd have a look at Boxted, which was a bit further on. A good bit further on, as it happened. And I had to walk back. *All* the way. Oh, my poor feet.' He groaned and waved them about in the air.

'Did you find anything?' Jan asked eagerly, unsympathetically pushing Nick's feet out of the way.

'Yes.' Nick sat bolt upright. 'I'm sure I've found your house. It's big and it's quite a way back from the road. But I crept near and I could see the marks, just like this, on the gable.' He pointed to the now faint scratch marks on his arm. 'It's got those fancy patterns on the plaster and the chimneys are just like you drew. I'm sure it's your house, Jan, absolutely sure. And if my poor feet weren't in such a state and it wasn't such a long way I'd take you there right now.'

Jan turned a somersault on the floor, covering himself with dust. 'We've found it! We've found it! We've found where my grandfather lives!' he chanted, capering round like a juggler at a fair.

'All right. Now go away and let me go to sleep. I'm worn right out.' Nick turned his back on Jan and pretended to be asleep with exaggerated snoring noises.

'No, no, you can't go to sleep.' Jan went over and shook him. 'Listen to this. I've got something to tell you, now.' And he told Nick about the message he'd been ordered to deliver to the "Woolpack" for Mynheer van Migrode.

'There's something I don't like about that man,' he said when he'd finished. 'He sends shivers down my spine.' He looked at Nick. 'Are there wild boar in Donyland Woods?'

'Oh, yes. My gran used to tell me the tale of how my grandad killed one there once. He waited in a tree till it came past and then he fell on it and stuck a knife in its neck.'

'Are they good to eat?'

'I reckon so.'

The boys were silent for a bit. Then Jan said. 'I don't think they're going to hunt wild boar at all, do you?'

'No. I reckon it's a person they're going to hunt.'

'I wonder who?'

'Perhaps it's Scarface,' Nick said in a hushed tone.

'No, it wouldn't be him, would it? He's on their side, dolt-head.'

'No, he isn't.'

'Yes, he is. We saw him at the old warehouse looking for Mynheer Verlender's Bible.'

'Oh, yes, so we did.' Nick screwed his face up anxiously. 'I wonder just what *is* going on.'

Jan sighed and shook his head. 'I don't know. I only wish we hadn't got mixed up in it. I don't want to take this message to the "Woolpack" but I suppose I must . . .' his voice trailed off, '. . . unless we go to my grandfather's house *instead*.' His face lit up. 'When I tell him who I am he'll take us in and shelter us and he'll have my mother and sister brought over from Holland and we'll never need to have anything to do with all this horrible war business again.'

Nick looked at him. 'Us?' he said, doubtfully. 'Shelter us?'

'Yes, of course.' Jan looked at him, surprised. 'You don't think I'd leave you out, do you? Not after all we've done together. Come on, let's go now.' He went to the door. 'Well, come on, Nick.'

Nick examined his feet. 'I don't think I could walk all that way and back twice in one day,' he said, shaking his head.

'But you won't have to! We've only got to walk one way! Once we get there, we'll *stay*!' Jan was almost beside himself with excitement.

Fortunately for Nick, they got a lift on a tumbril carrying turnips for most of the way and they only had to walk up the long straight road that led to Boxted village.

'Your grandfather must be very rich,' Nick said. 'It's a very big house. You'll see it in a minute, behind those trees.'

'My mother never talked about it, so I don't know,' Jan said. 'But the house looked pretty big from the picture, didn't it?'

'I wonder if there'll be real beds, with feather mattresses. My gran had a feather mattress. She used to let me lie on it when I was ill.' Nick turned aside into a little copse. 'Come on, it's quicker through here. Look, you can see the house now, through those trees. That's the one, isn't it?'

Jan looked and for a moment tears blurred his vision. There it was, right in front of him, the house in the picture he'd looked at so many times, the house he had come all this way to find. Now he'd found it, his grandfather's house. Now he would be safe, Nick would be safe, and soon his mother and Betkin would be brought to England and safety. He gulped.

'Yes, Nick,' he said. 'This is the house.'

Suddenly, from behind, they heard a low-throated growl, and before they could turn a hand grabbed each of them by the collar, lifting them right off the ground.

'What do you think you're after, you little sneak thieves?

Conies? Partridges? Or hopin' for better pickin's from the master's house?' An enormous man, with a big black dog growling at his side, looked at each of them in turn, holding them up as if they were no heavier than a couple of weasels.

'Put me down! Put me down!' Nick shouted, his feet flailing the empty air.

'We're not thieves. I've come to see my grandfather,' Jan yelled, half-strangled.

'Oh?' The man was quite roughly dressed in a leather jerkin and breeches, with a partridge feather in his cap. 'And who might your grandfather be?' He thrust his face right up to Jan's and Jan could smell the ale on his breath.

'He lives here,' he said.

'Where?'

'At that house.' Jan jerked his head as best he could in the direction of the big house.

'And what's your grandfather's name, might I ask?' The man, who looked as if he might be the gamekeeper, clearly didn't believe a word.

Jan bit his lip. 'I don't know,' he admitted.

'No, I don't suppose you do know what his name is because my master isn't your grandfather. My master hasn't got any grandchildren. In fact, my master hasn't got any children at all, that I know of.' He put the boys down, still holding them firmly by the scruff of their necks. 'You're lyin'. I can tell you're lyin'. You've come here to see what you can poach from my land. Well, I'm not havin' any of it. If I see you round these parts again I shall set the dog on you. An' I *mean* it!' He gave them both a shake, banging their heads together in the process. Then he lifted them up again and carried them through the wood, back to the road. 'There,' he said. 'Now, be off with you, back to wherever it is you came from. And don't let me see you anywhere near this place again.' He put the boys down and released them so suddenly that they fell against each other. 'An' don't you try any funny business, like tryin' to sneak in the back way. Rex here has got a very sharp nose and very sharp teeth,' he called after them as they stumbled up the road.

They ran and walked for nearly a mile before they dared to stop. Then they threw themselves down on the grass at the side of the road.

'Now what are we going to do?' Nick asked miserably.

Jan bit his lip very hard because he knew he could easily burst into tears. 'I don't know,' he said in a tight little voice.

'It *was* the right house, wasn't it?' Nick said.

Jan nodded, not trusting himself to speak.

'How on earth are we going to get to see your grandfather if that stupid gamekeeper won't let us anywhere near the place?'

Jan shrugged his shoulders and gave a loud sniff. 'I don't know,' he said again. He put his head down on his knees so that Nick shouldn't see the tears of disappointment that he could no longer hold back.

After a while, Nick said, 'Come on, let's go back home. I'll take you out for a sail in my little boat.'

Jan got to his feet. 'All right. We can't do anything else here, can we?' he said, with a watery smile. 'Anyway, Nick, thanks for coming with me.'

'Thass all right. I thought I was going to sleep on a feather mattress.' Nick tried to cover his own disappointment with this pathetic attempt at a joke.

They began to trudge the long road back to the dockside. As they went their natural optimism began to come back and they became more cheerful, thinking up schemes to gain access to the house that became more and more outlandish and impossible — from Nick luring the dog so that Jan could run to the house and burst into his grandfather's study, to setting on the gamekeeper and binding and gagging him — and his dog — and then forcing him to take them to his master.

After a while Jan became silent.

'What's the matter?' Nick asked.

'I've just realised. We came here instead of taking that message to the "Woolpack".'

71

Nick stopped in his tracks. 'Oh, Lord, so we did.'

The two boys looked at each other. 'It's an awful long way to the "Woolpack" from here,' Nick said, after a bit. 'And it's getting a bit late now.'

'But what shall I tell old Yellow Fangs?' Jan said desperately. 'He'll *kill* me if I don't go. Is there a short-cut?'

Nick shook his head. 'The shortest way is about five miles from here, I should think. It wasn't going to matter,' he said gloomily. 'We were going to be safe at your grandfather's house by now.'

'Well, we're not and it does matter.' Fear and anxiety were making Jan short-tempered. 'So, what am I going to do?'

Nick began to quicken his pace, hobbling a little on his sore feet. 'We'll just have to try and get to the "Woolpack" in time, that's all,' he said. 'But let's call in at my cabin on the way, we nearly have to pass it, anyway.'

'Why?'

'I've got some nice apples. I picked some for a lady the other day and she gave me a bagfull.'

'Oh, good. I'm so thirsty I could drink a well dry.'

They hurried along. There was a long walk ahead and not much time to do it in. Or so they thought. But when they went up the steps to the cabin and opened the door they found someone already there, waiting for them.

'Well, well, well,' said Scarface. 'And where do you think you've been all this time?'

SCARFACE

The two boys cowered back against the door and Jan felt the colour drain from his face. So someone already knew he hadn't been to the "Woolpack".

Scarface was sitting on the stool by the table, leaning against the wall. He seemed to be holding his arm rather awkwardly.

'Well?' Scarface repeated. 'Where do you think you've been all this time? I've been here hours waiting for you.'

The two boys looked at each other and Jan licked his lips. 'We've been to Boxted,' he croaked.

'Boxted? What have you been there for?' He leaned forward, gazing at them intently.

'Don't tell him,' Nick warned, giving Jan a kick.

But Jan wasn't going to tell him. Getting into that house of his grandfather's was his only chance of escape from the clutches of these people. He knew he was in terrible trouble over this "Woolpack" business so any likelihood of old Yellow Fangs rescuing his mother and sister was gone. Not that the fat Dutchman had so far shown any sign of keeping his promise to help them.

73

Scarface smiled. It was a crooked smile because the scar that stretched right down into his beard made his face stiff on one side. It made him look more like a pirate than ever. 'I think it's time we had a talk,' he said. 'And first of all I'd like you to tell me when you last saw your . . .' he hesitated, searching for the right word '. . . master, Jan.'

Jan thought for a minute. If Scarface and old Yellow Fangs were on the same side, and it would seem from the Bible business that they were, that couldn't do any harm. He hardly cared any more; anyhow, he was so tired and disappointed over the trip to Boxted. 'This morning,' he muttered in reply.

'And before that?'

The questions went on, relentlessly. What did Jan tell him? What did van Migrode reply? Did he make a note of things? Did Jan ever see him talking to anyone else?

At last Nick burst out. 'But if you're on his side you must know all these things. Why do you keep questioning Jan? He always does as he's told. Well, nearly always.'

'I'm questioning Jan to make sure he hasn't put any of my men's lives in danger while I've been away,' Scarface said tersely. 'I told you before to keep out of all this and I hoped to heaven you'd taken my advice, but it seems you chose to disregard it.' He shifted on the stool and the movement made him wince. 'Van Migrode is a nasty piece of work, and cunning with it. We've had our eye on him for some time, and at one time we thought he was the brains behind what's going on, but it could be that he's only doing as he's told and that the network stretches far beyond Colchester. And that's what I'm trying to find out!'

The two boys looked doubtful.

Scarface sighed. 'Shall I tell you exactly what you've got yourselves mixed up in?' He looked from one to the other, 'You still don't understand, do you?' The boys shook their heads and he went on, 'There's a group here in England who are engaged in smuggling. Smuggling not things, but people. They smuggle important people who have come to England to escape from Alva's cruel persecution — what's known as

74

the Spanish Inquisition — *back* to Holland so that they can be handed over to the Spanish authorities to be tortured and killed.'

'You mean they're working over here, in England, for the Spaniards?' Nick asked.

'That's right. Now you know what the war over here is all about, don't you?'

Once again the boys looked doubtful.

'Well, I'll tell you.' Once again Scarface moved and once again he winced.

'The people of the Netherlands are in revolt against Philip of Spain's government. Although there are many other things — like the tenth penny tax — which have caused discontent, the whole thing has divided itself into a religious war. A war between Spanish Catholics under the Duke of Alva and the Protestant Netherlands under the Prince of Orange. And of the Protestants the Calvinists are the fiercest fighters — the Anabaptists tend to simply lie down and die for their faith. Anyway, as you know, most of the people who have come here to Colchester are Calvinists. They escaped while they could, some of them with nothing more than the clothes they stood up in. Do you understand so far?'

The boys nodded and Jan bit his lip anxiously. He and his family were Protestants.

Scarface went on, 'England, of course, is in a rather delicate position. Our gracious Sovereign, Good Queen Bess, while she doesn't want to upset Philip of Spain if she can help it, won't refuse sanctuary to the Dutch refugees because they are skilled workers and will help to keep England prosperous. So there you have it, in a nutshell.'

Scarface looked round. 'Is there a mug of water anywhere?'

'In my bucket,' Nick said.

'Ugh, you can't give him that. You've put your head in it.' Jan made a face, he was watching Scarface intently.

'No I haven't, this is a fresh lot.' Nick dipped his mug in the bucket and gave it to Scarface.

'Thanks!' Scarface took a drink and put the mug down on the table. 'Well, to continue. Add to this little mixture the people who don't care which side wins as long as they themselves make a lot of money, the traitors who appear to be what they're not, the Sea Beggars who began on the side of the Prince of Orange fighting the Spanish but are now little more than pirates and brigands, terrorising land and sea alike, and a few people who simply try to find out what the next move is likely to be so that their government will be prepared, and it's no wonder nobody knows who to trust.'

'Where do you come in all this?' Nick said warily. 'You're English. Why should you —'

'I know where he comes in,' Jan said suddenly. '*I* know who you are. I've seen you before. Twice. Once in the "Pipe and Jar" and once on the quay.'

Scarface smiled at him and winked his eye. 'That's right.'

Then Jan was sure. 'You haven't really got a beard, nor that great ugly scar,' he said.

'No, you're quite right, I haven't.' Scarface put up his hand and with some difficulty peeled a corner of the scar away. Then he patted it back into place. 'It's a very useful disguise,' he said, with a lopsided smile.

'And it's just stuck on?' Nick's eyes were like saucers.

'Yes, with a particularly vile but tenacious fish glue.'

'But what's it made of?' Jan went up to him and peered closely at the scar.

'Oh, skin of various kinds. And I have a friend who is a very skilful dyer. He's made quite a realistic job of it — and my face round it for that matter — hasn't he?' he held his face up for examination.

'Whew, yes.' Jan backed away. 'You'd never know it wasn't real.'

'I may say it's the very deuce to get off,' Scarface said ruefully.

'But you still haven't told us who you are,' Nick persisted.

'I'm Philip Jardine, an officer in the Queen's Navy . . .'

'Ah, yes. That was what was odd about you when I saw you

76

the other day. You were wearing a cutlass at your belt instead of a sword. I remember now,' Jan said eagerly.

'Standard practice,' Philip told him. 'Since a sword is of limited use at close quarters on a boat.' He winced as he made an effort to stand up. 'I had a slight accident just over a week ago,' he explained. 'I haven't quite recovered from it.'

'Were *you* on the *Marigold*?' Jan asked. Everything seemed to be falling into place.

'Yes, I was. And we were lucky not to be sunk, I might tell you. There was a sloop waiting for us off Languard Point. We thought at first it was those brigands, the Sea Beggars, but then we realised it wasn't them at all. They would have boarded and robbed us, not opened fire and tried to sink us. We couldn't wait to see who it was, though, we had to turn tail for Harwich. You see, our ship wasn't armed and our cargo was too valuable to risk being lost — fifty of the best men in Colchester from the Dutch Quarter; hand picked to go and fight for the Prince of Orange.'

'Who was it then, if wasn't the Sea Beggars?' Jan asked.

'You tell me,' Philip said. 'It's plainly a secret underground movement to help the Spaniards, and it's well organised too. They somehow got wind of ship movements — and we know how they did that, don't we?' He cocked an eyebrow at Jan, 'And sent a ship to wait in the North Sea and sink us.'

'Yellow Fangs,' Jan breathed, horror stricken at the part he'd been playing.

'Yes, I'm afraid so, if that's what you call your friend Mynheer Abraham van Migrode.'

'Is that where you got hurt?' Nick asked.

Philip looked down at his shoulder. 'Yes, I got in the way of a piece of shot when those traitors tried to sink us. They damned nearly managed it, too. If our Captain hadn't known the waters so well and managed to run them aground so we could get away, none of us would be here to tell the tale.'

'Is that why Yellow Fangs wanted to know all the ship movements?' Jan said.

'That's one reason. Another is so that any valuable cargo can be

77

intercepted and pirated. They have to finance their little ventures, you understand, and it can be expensive.'

'The ruby boat,' the boys said together.

'That's right. They made a nice little haul that night.'

'And we thought it was you,' Jan said.

'We thought you were in league with the Sea Beggars,' Nick added.

Scarface threw back his head and laughed. 'Not me,' he said, 'I'm a highly respected servant of Her Majesty!'

'Then why do you need that disguise?' Nick said, quick as a flash.

'Because sometimes a highly respected servant of Her Majesty can be sent across the sea to find out what the situation is, so that he can report back what Philip of Spain's next move is likely to be and whether it is prudent to feign support. A character dressed like I am now is far more likely to glean information than an officer in the Queen's Navy.' He looked at them both sternly, 'But that little piece of information is *strictly* confidential.'

'Is he telling the truth, Jan?' Nick asked. He looked worried and perplexed.

'Yes, I'm sure he is,' Jan said firmly. 'And I'm glad now that we didn't go to the "Woolpack".'

Philip shot him a piercing glance. 'The "Woolpack"? Why were you supposed to go there?'

'To deliver a message. But it would be too late, anyway, by the time we got there.'

'What was the message?'

Jan closed his eyes to concentrate. 'Make ready for the hunting party. Tonight they're after the wild boar.'

'Is that all?'

'Yes, that's all.'

'And those are the exact words?'

'Yes. He made me repeat them to make sure I'd got them right.'

Philip sat deep in thought for a few minutes. Then he said, 'The "Woolpack" is out on the Donyland Road, isn't it?'

'Yes,' Nick answered this time. 'It's about three miles away on the edge of Donyland Wood.'

'Mm. So van Migrode is mixed up in that little operation, too. I didn't realise he was dabbling in that as well.'

'What?' Jan asked.

'Why, smuggling men wanted by the Spanish authorities back to Holland against their will.'

'Mynheer Verlender!' The boys looked at each other.

Philip raised his eyebrows. 'You know about that, too?'

'I saw it happen. Well, nearly,' Jan said. 'I've got Mynheer Verlender's Bible.'

'Have you indeed,' Philip said. 'Well, I think you'd better let me have that.'

'We thought that was what you were looking for that night at the old warehouse. That's why we thought you were mixed up with old Yellow Fangs,' Nick said.

'No, we'd had word that something was likely to happen there and I had gone to investigate. But they'd changed the plan and gone three days earlier.' Philip sighed and shook his head at the two boys. 'You're lucky you haven't found yourselves hanging on the end of a rope,' he said in an exasperated tone. 'I told you not to get yourselves mixed up in all this.'

The boys hung their heads. Then Jan's curiosity got the better of him.

'So Mynheer Verlender was taken back to Holland?' he said. 'I wasn't sure. I thought perhaps they'd drowned him.'

'It would probably have been better for the poor man if they had.' Philip got awkwardly to his feet. 'However, we can't do anything for him now, but we can try and head off the wild boar, whoever he is. There's still time, it won't be dark for another two hours and they'll not make a move in daylight, that's for sure.'

'What can we do?' the boys asked together.

'Well, first of all, Jan, you must deliver the message exactly as you've been told to. I'll help you along part of the way, but you'll have to do the last bit on foot. The rest you must leave to me.' He gazed at Jan as if weighing him up. Then he said, 'In doing this, Jan, you realise you'll be putting yourself in danger? If van Migrode discovers you've told me his plans he won't hesitate to have you disposed of.'

Jan nodded. He'd already realised that.

'But that's not all. There are other things I need to know in order to bring these ruffians to the gallows. Things that you will be able to find out and tell us that we wouldn't be able to discover any other way. Will you do as I won't remind you I asked you to some weeks ago? Will you pass the same information to me as you do to Mynheer van Migrode? Tell Nick what you discover and I will contact him — I don't want to be seen talking to you, Jan. Find out van Migrode's movements, where he goes, who he sees. We must find out who the head of this organisation is. Go to his house if necessary.'

'I was there once, he was furious!'

'Well, you may have to go there again. You're little and wiry, you can hide in dark corners. I'll warn you, it will be dangerous work, more dangerous than anything you've done so far.' He turned to Nick. 'And you will be in it as much as Jan from now on,' he said grimly. 'Well, will you do it?'

THE WOOLPACK

The boys looked at each other and then at Philip. 'Yes,' they both said together. 'We'll do it.'

'Good lads. Now, there's no time to waste. Start walking to the "Woolpack". You'll be picked up before you've gone half a mile. I think I know who the "wild boar" is likely to be. I must try and get someone to warn him. All right?'

'All right.' The boys nodded.

'One more thing. We need some kind of signal.' Philip looked round the cabin. 'Ah, I know.' He pointed to Nick's bucket of water. 'When you've got something to tell me, put your bucket outside on the top step. If it's very urgent turn it upside down. Do you understand?'

'Yes. Put the bucket out if there's news. Turn it upside down if it's urgent,' Nick said. 'And if you don't want to be seen coming here you can always use the back way.'

'Better than ever.' Philip nodded approvingly. 'How?'

'I'll show you. I don't often use it nowadays because everyone knows that I live here and they don't mind. But when I first made my cabin I used to sneak in and out so nobody knew. This way.'

Carefully, Nick removed a board from the end of the cabin and they all stepped through into the upper floor of the sail loft. Below, they could see a sail chalked out on the floor and a roll of canvas near it, together with a box of cringles, reels of twine and sailmaker's plans. Across the loft another board had to be removed and they stepped through into an adjoining warehouse, this one full of dyestuffs, with vats and barrels and great bundles of weed-like looking vegetables. 'Mind, you have to step down here. It pongs a bit, too,' Nick warned. Across this floor yet another board came out to take them through to the loft of a disused boat shed, down the steps and out through a door in the side that gave on to an alleyway leading back to the quay.

'Couldn't be better,' Philip said. 'Now, off you go. Someone will pick you up before long. Mind how you go, and good luck.'

'You see, I *knew* Scarface wasn't a rogue,' Nick said smugly as they hurried along. 'Oh, my poor feet. I'd forgotten they were so sore.' He began to hobble.

'Never mind, Scarf . . . Philip said we'd be picked up before long.'

Just then an old cart went past them, carrying a load of straw. A little way past them it rumbled to a halt.

'Goin' my way?' the old be-smocked farmer shouted over his shoulder. 'I can take yer as far as Old Heath.'

The boys drew level. Travelling with this old man wouldn't be much quicker than walking.

'You ain't likely to find much else along this road to help yer along,' the farmer said, looking straight ahead and chewing rhythmically on a piece of straw.

After a moment's hesitation the boys clambered up beside him.

'Goin' far?' the farmer asked. He had his hat pulled down over his ears and a few wispy grey hairs hung below it.

'No, not far,' Jan said. 'Old Heath will do fine.'

Just then a horse and rider galloped by at a cracking pace, nearly frightening the old farmer's nag off the road. Nick and

Jan exchanged glances. That must have been the horse Philip had sent to pick them up. But they were careful to say nothing.

The old farmer wanted to know all about them, where they lived and where they were going. Were they going visiting and why were they out at this time of day when it would soon be dark?

Both boys were careful not to give anything away in their answers and wished they'd soon reach Old Heath.

Suddenly, the old farmer looked at them and winked.

'Philip!' Jan said, recognising him.

'Ssh!' Philip whispered. He smiled, 'Well, I must say you stood up well to my questioning. You didn't give a thing away.'

'I thought what a nosey old man you were,' Nick said. 'I didn't realise you were testing us out.'

'You must always be on your guard,' Philip warned.

They rumbled on, past Old Heath and on to the Donyland Road.

'Now,' Philip said, 'I'll have to put you down in a minute, Jan, and you'll have to walk the rest of the way. Remember, you've walked *all* the way and you've hurried because you know there's not much time, so you'll be tired and a bit out of breath. I'll take Nick with me to hide this cart somewhere so that the old nag can crop the grass.'

'Where shall I meet you?' Jan said.

'You won't meet me. I shall go round to the back of the inn to keep watch, but I want you two to stay at the front. That way we'll be able to see everything that goes on. Not that anything will go on if my man has been in time. But if he hasn't ... Anyway, you'll find a big oak tree next to the inn near the road and there's a ditch running beside it. And that's where you'll find Nick. Do you understand? He'll be hidden in the bracken.'

'Yes, I understand.' Jan nodded.

'But don't go straight to him,' Philip warned. 'Remember,

you've come from Colchester and that's where you'll be return-
ing to. You must go some way along the road before you double
back. The undergrowth is pretty thick by the side of the road so
you shouldn't have any problems.'

'You think of everything, Philip, don't you?' Nick said,
admiringly.

'I need to in my job, if I want to stay alive. Now, off you
go, Jan. And good luck.'

Jan climbed down and the cart rumbled on, to be concealed
deep in Donyland Wood.

The landlord at the "Woolpack" was a swarthy man with
broad shoulders and greenish eyes that gazed most of the time
at each other.

'Left it pretty late, ain't yer?' he said, when Jan had given him
the message between great gulps of breath. 'How's 'e expect me
ter be ready in less than 'arf a hour?'

'I missed the road,' Jan lied.

'Well, don't miss it on the way back.' The landlord put his
face menacingly close to Jan's. 'An' don't you 'ang about. There's
wolves in that there wood an' they eat little whippersnappers
like you.'

Jan hurried off down the road, looking back to make sure the
landlord was still watching him. He'd gone nearly half a mile
before he felt it safe to dive into the undergrowth and make his
way back to Nick.

Nick was carefully hidden in the ditch under the oak tree.
'It's a bit scratchy,' he warned as Jan settled down beside
him.

'Where's Philip?' Jan asked.

'He's down the other end of the ditch where he can watch
the stables.'

'I can't see him.'

'You're not supposed to be able to see him, clumphead.'

'Has anything happened?'

'Yes. Three men on horses have gone off through the woods
towards Mersea. One went, then a little while later another one

84

followed him. The last one's only just gone. He was riding one horse and leading another.'

'Listen.' Jan cocked his ear. 'I can hear horses' hooves. Perhaps they're coming back.'

As they watched a coach and pair came hurtling out of the wood and careered off towards Colchester.

'That'll be the Mersea coach,' Nick said. 'It runs twice a week. But not usually as fast as that.'

'Do you reckon that was what they meant by the "wild boar"?' Jan said excitedly.

'No, I reckon the "wild boar" was going to be on the coach.' Nick shifted his position. 'It's getting dark. I hope we'll be able to see if anything happens.'

'Ssh. Someone's coming.'

They watched, keeping their heads well down, and after a few minutes three men on horseback emerged from the wood, leading a fourth horse by the bridle.

'They're the ones who went out,' Nick whispered.

'Take the 'orses, Joe,' one said. 'We'll get 'im inside, quick.'

'That's the landlord. I recognise his voice,' Jan whispered.

'Who do they mean, "him"?' Nick whispered back. 'Oh, look! They've got something hanging over the saddle of that horse they were leading.'

'It's a man. Philip's messenger must have been too late,' Jan breathed.

One man, who looked as if he was a kind of servant, or ostler, led three of the horses round to the stables at the back, while the landlord and the other man, who was very tall and thin, untied the captive, who looked like nothing more than a bundle of cloth draped over the saddle, except that his hands and feet were tied together under the horse's belly. Then the landlord rapped on the door. 'Open up, Lizzie!' he called, and there was the sound of bolts being drawn back.

The tall, thin man lifted the limp body from the horse and almost threw it over his shoulder. 'Come on, my fine friend. Up you come,' he said.

The man had spoken in Dutch and, recognising the words, Jan gave an involuntary cry. Quickly, Nick clapped his hand over his friend's mouth.

'What was that? I heard a noise,' the landlord said, looking over his shoulder.

'It was nothing,' the Dutchman said with a heavy accent. 'You're imagining things.'

'I'm not so sure.' The landlord picked up a cudgel and walked over to the other side of the road. Satisfying himself that there was nothing there he came over to where the two boys were hidden and began beating the undergrowth with the cudgel. Jan and Nick kept perfectly still, their mouths dry and their hearts thumping so hard that they feared he would hear.

'No, you're right, there ain't nothin' there.' The cudgel came down again, missing Nick's head by an inch, before the landlord turned away and followed the Dutchman and his bundle into the "Woolpack" and closed the door.

'Whew!' Nick let out a long sigh of relief. 'That was a near thing.'

'Yes, but don't you realise,' Jan said, 'that was the man!'

'What man?' Nick said. He didn't know what his friend was talking about.

'That tall, thin man was the man I heard at the old warehouse and at old Yellow Fangs' house. That Dutchman! "My fine friend" — that's what he always says.'

Jan was almost beside himself with agitation and excitement.

'Ssh. Keep your voice down. Someone'll hear,' Nick warned.

'Three times I've heard him speak; I want to get a good look at him and see what he looks like.' Jan began to crawl forward. 'I'm going to creep to the window and have a look inside.'

Before he could move a hand was put over his mouth. 'You're not going anywhere, my lad. You're staying right here.' Philip's voice whispered in a tone that brooked no disobedience. 'Now, quiet, both of you, and follow me to where we can talk.'

He slid silently back the way he'd come through the undergrowth and the boys followed, making as little noise as they possibly could, their hands and breeches torn by brambles as they went. When he considered they were far enough from the "Woolpack" Philip stopped. 'There,' he said. 'We can talk here, and I can still keep my eye on the "Woolpack". Now, have you seen anything?'

'Oh, yes,' the boys said together. 'We saw . . .'

'One at a time.' Philip held up his hand. 'I can't listen if you both talk at the same time.'

So the boys took it in turns to tell their story and Philip listened, adding a question or remark here and there. 'Yes,' he said at one point, 'I saw the ostler stable the horses. Go on.'

When they had finished he stroked his chin, which in this disguise was covered in a grey stubble, and sat silent for some while. 'So we've got the landlord, the ostler, "my fine friend" the Dutchman, and the landlord's wife in there at the moment. Plus a prisoner who is tied up and may or may not have regained consciousness by this time.'

'What are we going to do?' Jan asked.

'Get him out of course. What else?' Philip grinned in the moonlight and for a moment they discerned the man behind the disguise. 'Now, I'm going to get the cart and drive right up to the inn and go inside for a draught of ale and some bread and cheese. While I'm inside I'll find out where our man is. You two keep watch to make sure he isn't taken away while I'm gone. It'll be best if you watch from the back, Nick, to make sure they don't get him away over the fields!'

It wasn't long before Philip was back. He tethered the horse very near to where Jan was crouching and went off into the inn. He seemed to be gone a very long time and when he came out he was carrying a leather bucket. 'Thank you, landlord. I always reckon to give the old hoss a drink when I have one meself,' he said in a quavering sort of voice. He brought the bucket over to the horse. 'Are you there, Jan?' he whispered, with his back to him.

'Yes.'

'Now, listen, because I shall only tell you once. They've got their prisoner upstairs, I'm sure of it. I've heard movements up there when the rest of them have been in sight. Anyway, I can see there's nowhere for them to put him downstairs. I suggest Nick climbs this oak tree. It overhangs the house and he can easily drop down on to the roof. He'll be able to hang on to the pegs that hold the thatch to work his way round to that dormer window at the front. I think he'll be able to open it by putting his hand through the lattice — there's no glass in any of the windows. Tell him to be *very quiet*. Every movement can be heard from downstairs. I'll act drunk and start to sing loudly if necessary. Got all that?'

'Yes.'

'Right. Now, what happens next will depend on what Nick finds. But if he can get the man out of the window and across the roof it'll be an easy matter to drop from the kitchen roof to the ground and get away. When I come out again for the bucket you must tell me if they've managed it. If they haven't I'll have to go in myself. But if they get away tell them to start walking. We'll pick them up as we pass. Got that?'

'Yes.'

'Good. Don't let anyone see you.' He went back to the inn. As he went Jan saw him flex his shoulder, the only indication he'd allowed himself of his painful wound.

'He's a slow drinker, my old hoss,' Jan heard him say as he went back inside. 'I reckon thass cos 'e ain't got no teeth ter chew the water.'

Nick listened carefully as Jan repeated Philip's instructions and lost no time in carrying them out. By the time Jan got back to his hiding place Nick had already opened the lattice and disappeared inside. But it seemed a very long time before he came out again and the window was a tight squeeze for the man he had with him. For a moment Jan saw them silhouetted on the roof against the moonlit sky and then they disappeared. A moment later he saw two shadowy figures glide from the dark bulk of the inn into the bushes beyond.

After a while the door of the inn opened. There was an

awful singing noise and Philip reeled out. 'I'll just fesh yer bucket lan'lord,' he said, 'an' then me an' th'ole hoss'll be yon our way.'

'I hope your old hoss knows the way,' the landlord shouted after him. 'For I reckon you're too drunk to find it.'

'My ole hoss'll take me home, don't you worry,' Philip shouted, then dropped his voice. 'Have they gone?' he whispered to Jan in his usual tone.

'Yes. Five minutes ago,' Jan whispered back.

'Get in the cart while I take this bucket back.' Philip raised his voice and staggered back across the road. 'Here y'are, lan'lord, the owd hoss drunk nearly as much as his master.' He reeled back and after three attempts climbed up into the cart.

They hadn't gone far before they drew level with the two walking along the road.

'Well done, Nick,' Philip said, as they helped them up beside them.

'It would have been a lot easier if he could have understood what I was talking about,' Nick grumbled. 'He can't speak any English at all. You ought to have gone, Jan.'

But Jan was deep in conversation with Mynheer van Ryke and wasn't listening. After a while he said, 'Philip, Mynheer van Ryke helped to organise those men to go over to Holland to fight, you know, the ones on the *Marigold*. He says that's why he was captured. He says if he'd been sent back to Holland he would have been roasted alive.'

'I'm sure he's right,' Philip nodded.

'He says he's worried about the other men who helped him. There was one from Coggeshall and one from Halstead.'

'Ah,' Philip said. 'That all fits in with what I heard tonight at the "Woolpack" when they thought I was drunk.'

'What did you hear?' the boys both asked together.

'Well, the Dutchman said "That's one in the bag. Two more to come." Then the landlord said something like "I hope they'll be here early. We don't want this business hanging about", so the Dutchman said, "Don't worry. They'll be gone by Friday night".' Philip frowned. 'It was something like that but they spoke in whispers and I had to keep singing to pretend I was drunk.'

'You were very good,' Jan said. 'I almost thought you were drunk.'

'Friday is the day after tomorrow,' Nick said.

'Yes. Now, the first thing I must do is get Mynheer van Ryke to safety. Then, tomorrow, I'll go and see the magistrate and get a warrant to arrest the landlord of the "Woolpack".'

Jan tugged his sleeve. 'Can I come along with you, Philip?'

'What, to the "Woolpack"? No, indeed you can't, my lad,' Philip said firmly.

'No, I mean to see the magistrate. He might be able to help me reach my grandfather.'

'Oh, yes, I don't see any problem there.' Philip smiled at him. 'I'm sure Sir John can help you. He knows just about everybody in the district.'

But when they arrived at the magistrate's house the next morning Sir John Dalrymple was out and the servant said he wouldn't be back that day.

THE VISIT

Jan was disappointed. He had brushed his clothes carefully for the visit and had scrubbed his face and hands until they were quite sore. And now it was all wasted.

'I suppose I'll have to find some other way of getting into my grandfather's house,' he said, as Philip swung him up into the saddle with him.

'Do you know where it is, then?' Philip asked.

'Oh, yes. I've been there. I went yesterday. But the gamekeeper wouldn't let me in.'

'Where is this house?'

'Over on the Boxted Road. It's a long walk.'

'But it won't take long on horseback.' He turned his horse's head. 'And the gamekeeper won't refuse me entrance, I'll be bound.'

Boxted didn't seem very far at all travelling on Philip's big black stallion and Jan felt a thrill of satisfaction to see the big gamekeeper touch his forelock and make no attempt to stop them as they cantered up the wide avenue between the trees.

The house was as familiar to him as if he'd lived there all his life and the initials in the pargeting, JCR, were quite plain. This was his grandfather's house. Already he felt he belonged here. Philip rapped on the door and a servant showed them into a large hall, open to the rafters, with a gallery at one end.

'I'm afraid the master's away, sir, but his godson, Mr Rupert, is here. One moment, I'll tell him you're here.'

Rupert came out of a small study adjoining the hall. He was a young man of not much over twenty with a pale face and rather sullen expression.

'I'm afraid Sir Joshua Rawlings is away in London,' Rupert said. He didn't look very pleased at being disturbed.

'When will he be back?' Philip asked politely.

'Not until after the weekend.'

'Then perhaps you can help us. You are Sir Joshua's godson?'

'That's right. And heir to his estate.'

'Oh.' Philip was taken slightly aback. 'But what about his daughter?'

'He hasn't got a daughter and his son is dead. He hasn't got any family. I'm his sole heir.'

'That's very odd,' Philip said. 'This young man with me is sure that this house belongs to his grandfather.'

'Rubbish. Utter and complete nonsense,' Rupert said rudely in a loud voice.

The door of the study opened and another man came out. To Jan's surprise it was Sir John Dalrymple. 'What's going on, Rupert?' he asked. He had a glass of wine in his hand and his speech was a little bit slurred. 'Ah, good morning, Jardine, my good man,' he said, catching sight of Philip. 'What brings you here?'

'Good fortune, it would seem, Sir John,' Philip bowed his head to the older man, 'since I particularly wanted to see you. Your servant said you were out and wouldn't be back today.'

'No. Quite right. Quite right. I'm spending the day here with Rupert, my nephew. What did you want to see me about?'

Philip looked about him. 'I'd prefer to talk to you privately, Sir John, if you don't mind.'

'Very well. Come into the study.'

The two men went in and closed the door. Rupert sat down with one leg draped over the arm of his chair and looked Jan up and down.

'You impudent young puppy,' he said. 'How dare you come here and pretend to be Sir Joshua's grandson. Who put you up to it? Are you planning to share the estate half and half with whoever your confederate is?'

Jan twisted his cap in his hands nervously. He didn't like this man Rupert very much. 'I don't know what you mean, sir,' he said, careful of his manners. 'I've come to see my grandfather.'

'Is Philip Jardine in it with you? I shouldn't be surprised if he was. I never did trust that man.' Rupert got to his feet and began pacing up and down. 'Where did he find you, eh? Tell me, where did he find you?' He came over to Jan, picked him up by the shoulders and began to shake him.

'I don't know. I don't know what you're talking about. Please, put me down,' Jan cried.

Rupert put him down so roughly that he fell on the floor. He had only just got to his feet when the study door opened. 'Bring me ink and a quill and some sand,' they heard Sir John roar from inside the room as Philip came out. A few moments later Sir John followed him.

'There you are, my boy,' Sir John said, handing Philip a paper rolled and sealed with wax. 'That's all you'll need to round them up and take them — um, let me see, yes, take them to the castle, that'll be the safest place. They'll be out of harm's way there and we'll be able to question them and find out just what's going on.' He turned to Rupert. 'What's the matter with you, my boy? You don't look very pleased with life.'

Rupert laughed. 'Oh, nothing's the matter with me, uncle. It's just that this silly little boy has come here claiming to be Sir Joshua's grandson.'

'What a preposterous idea. Sir Joshua's son was killed when he was seventeen. He wasn't even married,' Sir John said.

'But my mother . . . his daughter,' Jan protested.

'He never had a daughter,' Rupert said quickly. 'Did he, uncle?'

'Not that I ever knew of,' Sir John agreed.

'But look, I've got a lucky medallion.' Desperately, Jan tore off his medallion and gave it to them. Sir John looked at it briefly. 'Colchester cloth seal. Hundreds of 'em about. Doesn't mean a thing.'

Jan's eyes filled with tears as he took his medallion back. Was he never going to find his grandfather? He felt Philip's hand on his shoulder. 'Come along, lad. You've obviously made a mistake. You must have the wrong house.'

But Jan knew differently. He knew it was his grandfather's house. So what was going on?

UP THE CREEK

When Jan returned to the "Pipe and Jar" it was closed. That was unusual. Silas would never lose the opportunity to make a few pence. Jan went to find Nick. He was getting the boat ready to go fishing.

'Oh, yes,' Nick said, 'Emily came to leave a message. They've taken some pies and pasties to sell at St Denis's Fair on Magdalen Green. You're to go as soon as you get back so that you can help Emily while Silas comes back to open the "Pipe and Jar".' He dropped his voice. 'Emily said she wouldn't bother if she was you!' he said with a grin.

Jan looked longingly at Nick's little boat. 'I don't suppose I'd find them in amongst the crowd anyway, would I?' he said hopefully.

'No,' Nick said, 'I'm sure you wouldn't.'

'It's getting late, too,' Jan said.

'Yes,' Nick agreed. After a bit Nick said, 'I'm going out in my boat to catch some fish.'

'That'll be nice,' Jan said, kicking a stone into the water.

'I expect Silas would like a nice fish for supper. He's very fond of fish, I believe.'

'Yes, he is.'

'Why don't you come with me and catch some for him?'

Before Nick had finished speaking Jan was down the iron pegs in the quayside that formed steps down to the water and into the boat. 'What a good idea,' he said with a grin.

'You're looking very smart,' Nick said as he cast off. 'And clean! I didn't realise you'd got freckles.'

'Philip took me to see my grandfather. But there's something odd. Something I don't understand, going on.' Jan trailed his hand in the water and watched the pattern of ripples as he told Nick what had happened.

'P'raps your grandfather's moved. P'raps he doesn't live there any more,' Nick suggested.

'Yes, Philip said it must be the wrong house,' Jan nodded. 'That must be the answer, grandfather must have moved. But where on earth do we begin to look for him?'

The boys fell silent. Nick put up his little lugsail and the boat sailed gently down river. It was a busy river, with cargo boats, fishing boats and passenger boats all trying to use the narrow channel; the smaller ones trying to avoid being pushed aground by those bigger and more ruthless. Nick kept well in to the shore. His little boat had a very shallow draught and could skim over the treacherous mud that lay only inches below the surface in some places. They sailed on for some time, trailing a fishing line over the stern.

Then, 'I've brought my telescope,' Nick said importantly. 'I always like to keep an eye open to see what's going on.'

'But it's no good. I thought you said it was broken.'

'It's not *very* broken. Only a bit.' Nick took it from where it had been wrapped carefully in some sacks at the bottom of the boat and put it to his eye.

'Either it's broken or it isn't. It can't be a *bit* broken,' Jan said crossly. He was getting fed up. The boat wasn't really big enough for two and he was feeling cramped. They hadn't caught any fish either and it was beginning to rain.

'Here, you have a look. You'll see.' Nick handed Jan the telescope.

Jan took it without enthusiasm and put it to his eye. He wasn't good at closing one eye and he had to hold it shut with his finger, which didn't improve his temper. He swept it quickly round and handed it back to Nick.

Then he realised what he had seen.

'Quick, give it back,' he said. He put it to his eye again. 'That's it! That's the boat,' he said, nearly capsizing Nick's little dinghy in his excitement.

'Where? What boat?' Nick grabbed the telescope although really he could see just as well with his naked eye.

'Over there. In that creek. Can't you see it?' Jan pointed to a boat moored well up the creek. It had a very long bowsprit and an unusual shaped hull, but there was nothing else particularly odd about it.

'Yes, I can see it. What's wrong with it?'

'That's the boat! That's the boat they took Mynheer Verlender away on. Don't you remember? I saw it moored just below New Hythe docks.'

'Is it? Is it really the one? Have another look through the telescope to make sure.' Nick handed Jan the telescope. The boat was beginning to rock dangerously with their excited activity.

'I'm quite sure.' Jan handed back the telescope and the boys sat and looked at each other. Gradually, the boat stopped rocking and simply lifted gently on the tide.

'What do you think we should do?' Nick asked.

Jan thought for a bit. It was raining harder now, a thin grey drizzle. 'I suppose we ought to tell Philip.'

'Where is he?'

'I don't know.'

Nick shook his head. 'By the time we've put the bucket out and he's seen it and we've told him the boat's here, it'll have gone. No, *I* think we should go up the next creek and go ashore. Then we'll be able to crawl over that island till we get near enough to see who's on the boat and what they're up to.'

'But it's raining. We'll get wet.'

Nick gave him a scathing glance. 'Afraid of getting your face washed twice in one day?' he said. He groped in the bottom of the boat. 'Here,' he said. 'Here's a sack. It's open all down one side. Put it over your head. It'll be as good as a cloak.' He demonstrated with a second sack after he had taken down the lugsail and paddled the boat gently into the bank.

'There,' he said, tying the painter to an old iron stake. 'It'll be safe enough there. Come on, let's go and see what we can find out.'

'Don't forget this.' Jan handed him the telescope and followed him.

They managed to get quite close to the place where the boat was moored and they hid in the reeds and took it in turns to look through the telescope.

'There's nobody there,' Jan said. 'Nobody at all.'

'They won't keep popping up on deck, dunderhead. It's raining. They're probably having their tea.'

'I wish I was having mine,' Jan said. 'I'm starving. *And* soaking wet. Let's go. It's getting dark.'

'Not yet. We've only been here half an hour.'

'What do you expect to happen, for goodness sake?' Jan raised a bedraggled head and looked at his friend.

'Keep your head down. It's happening now.' Nick pushed Jan's face down into the reeds. Slowly, both boys raised their heads again.

There was a rhythmic plop of oars as a long, heavy rowing boat appeared out of the misty rain rowing towards the big boat. Four men appeared on the deck of the big boat and one of them let down a rope ladder. The rowing boat glided to a halt and they heard a voice, speaking in Dutch, say, 'Up you go, my fine fellows, one at a time now. Nice and easy. And don't try any funny business or you'll get a head full of lead-shot.'

'It's the voice. It's the same man!' Jan squealed.

'Quiet, they'll hear you,' Nick dug him in the ribs. He leaned over. 'Those must be the other two they were out to catch the other night,' he whispered.

'Can we rescue them?'

'I can't see how. There are four men that we've seen on the big boat and two men rowing the boat as well as the Voice and another man. That's at least eight that we know of. What could we do against that many?'

Jan sighed. 'No, you're right. But at least we'll be able to report to Philip what's happened.'

'Yes. Look — they've got the two men on board now. We'd better make ourselves scarce. Now, keep low as you go. We've got to get right across to the other side of the island to our boat.'

The two boys made off across the island, crouching as low as they could. Halfway across Nick stopped. 'I've left my telescope. I'm going back for it. You carry on and get the painter untied.' He ran back into the gloom, bent almost double, and Jan hurried on to where the little dinghy was tied. Jan untied the painter and waited. The tide was going out fast, and already the water was leaving the little boat. He wished Nick would hurry.

Then he heard a cry, faint but quite plain. 'After him, lads.' It was the Voice. 'Put Ben ashore to chase him. We'll go round the island in the boat and head him off.'

Jan could do nothing but wait, watching the water receding further and further, leaving Nick's little boat sitting on the mud.

Nick appeared. 'Quick, jump in,' he yelled.

Jan jumped in and Nick, perfectly at home on the river, gave the boat a push and skated along on the mud behind it until it floated. Then he jumped in and began to row.

'There they are!' The big rowing boat loomed out of the misty gloom.

'They'll have us cornered,' Jan yelled. 'You're taking us further up the creek.'

'I know what I'm doing,' Nick said, breathless from rowing. 'That's it, come on, follow me, a bit closer, a bit closer. That's it. That's done it.'

He swung his little boat round and began to row the other

way. Now Jan could see what his purpose had been. The two men on the oars were pulling with all their strength but the long, heavy boat wasn't moving an inch.

'They're stuck in the mud!' Jan said gleefully. 'They can't move.'

As he watched, the men stuck the oars upright and tried to pole the boat off; then one of them jumped in the water to try and push it off but he sank into the black, evil-smelling slime up to his waist and had to be hauled back over the side.

'Ha!' Nick said as they rowed past, close enough to hear the abuse that was being hurled at them but not close enough to risk being caught. 'They'll be there for the next six hours until the tide rises and floats them off again.'

'I got a good look at the Voice,' Jan said. He shook his head. 'He's ugly, Nick. Oh, he's ugly.'

'I'll bet he's in an ugly temper, too!' Nick was full of high spirits.

But Jan wasn't so happy. 'I keep thinking of those poor prisoners,' he said. 'I wonder what'll happen to them?'

'We'll tell Philip,' Nick said seriously, 'and hope we can do something before it's too late.'

'And I'd better get back to the "Pipe and Jar" before it's too late,' Jan said anxiously.

Silas gave him a good cuff as soon as he walked into the "Pipe and Jar". 'Where've you bin, you varmit? Mynheer van Migrode has bin waitin' ter see you this past hour. You'd better git yourself in that room. And don't forget to tell 'im you're sorry you kept 'im waitin'.'

Jan wiped the mud off his hands and went into the private room Silas always reserved for the wealthy Dutchman.

Whatever could old Yellow Fangs want at this hour of the day?

A VISIT TO AUNT ABIGAIL

Abraham van Migrode smiled as Jan entered the room and Jan heaved a sigh of relief to see that at least he wasn't in a bad temper.

'I've been away for a few days,' he said, 'so I fear I may be a bit out of touch with the comings and goings. What have you got to tell me, my boy?'

Jan thought for a minute. Truth to tell he'd been so pre-occupied with other things that he was finding difficulty in remembering. He cast his eye out of the window. The *Martha* was tied up to the quay and so was the *Jane*. The *Good Fortune* was just on her way down river on the last tide.

'The *Martha*'s in with a cargo of dyestuffs from London,' he said. 'And the *Jane*'s brought sea-coal down from Newcastle.' He leaned forward. 'The *Good Fortune* is off — to Spain, I think it is, and she's *supposed* to be carrying fleeces.' He nodded, knowing-ly, at the rich Dutchman. As far as Jan knew the *Good Fortune* was carrying fleeces and nobody had suggested otherwise, but it all helped to add an air of intrigue, and Jan wasn't averse to that.

'Ah!' Yellow Fangs nodded knowingly back. 'Good boy. Good boy. Keep me informed. Is there anything else?'

Jan leaned forward again. 'You've heard that the Sea Beggars have captured The Brill in the name of the Prince of Orange?' The Brill was a little town at the entrance to the lower Rhine and strategically important.

An ugly expression crossed van Migrode's face. 'Yes,' he snapped. 'I've heard that.' He composed his face again and patted Jan on the head, a gesture the boy had grown to hate. 'I'll come and see you again next week.'

The next morning Silas sent Jan to the market and while he was out he called at Nick's cabin. The bucket was outside, turned upside down.

'Has Philip called?' Jan asked.

'No, not yet. I don't know where he is. I've turned the bucket upside down so he'll know it's urgent,' Nick replied.

Just then there was a noise, a bit like scrabbling rats, and the board at the end of the cabin began to move. Then Philip appeared. He looked as if he hadn't been to bed.

'Well,' he said, almost before he was inside the cabin. 'What's happened? And it had better be important because I've no time to waste on things that don't matter, today. I've got some real trouble on my hands.'

As quickly as they could the boys told Philip about their trip down the river and seeing the prisoners taken aboard the strangely shaped boat.

'Which direction did they bring the prisoners from?' Philip asked when they had finished.

'Somewhere between Wyvenhoe and Brightlingsea. From the woods there, I should think. There are lots of little creeks they could have taken the boat into,' Nick said.

'Hm.' Philip stood leaning against the wall, resting his elbow on one hand, his chin sunk deep in the other. 'I'll have to organise some way of freeing them when they reach the other side. It's too late to get them off before they leave. You say the boat was a funny shape? Anything else strange about it?'

'It had an enormous bowsprit,' Nick said.

'Yes, it was like a great tree-trunk sticking out of the front of the boat,' Jan added.

'Good.' Philip nodded. 'Now, I've got to go to London on the evening coach tonight. I should be able to get a message to my men over the other side to watch out for it and do the necessary.'

'London?' the boys said together. 'Why have you got to go there?'

Philip looked at them for a long moment as if trying to make up his mind. Then he sat down on Nick's stool and gave a heavy sigh. 'Well, I suppose you might as well know, since you're in this business almost as deeply as I am. I went to the "Woolpack" last night. I realised that it was unlikely that those other two men would be taken there after the prisoner they'd got had been allowed — as they thought — to escape. But there was a chance. But what I didn't expect was to find the landlord and his wife and the ostler all lying there with their throats slit.'

The two boys gasped and almost as if a string had been released from the top of their heads they slid into a sitting position on the floor, never taking their eyes off Philip's face.

'Who did that?' Nick asked when he got his voice back.

'I don't know,' Philip said slowly. 'Of course, it may have been Jan's ugly Dutch friend — what do you call him — the Voice. He could have murdered them in a fit of temper because they'd let the prisoner get away.'

'He was in the boat with the other prisoners,' Jan said. 'We saw him.'

'Yes. The other two men must have been taken somewhere else when news got through of our man's escape.' Philip pinched his lip. 'Of course, there is another explanation.'

The two boys frowned.

'Well,' Philip explained, 'if the news leaked out that I was planning to arrest the landlord at the "Woolpack", *somebody* might have thought it safer to kill him first so that he wouldn't be able to talk.'

'But nobody knew except us, and we haven't told anybody,' Jan said.

Philip shot him a glance. 'You didn't breathe a word to van Migrode?' he asked.

'Of course I didn't,' Jan said indignantly.

'Have you spoken to anyone?' Philip turned to Nick.

'Only Captain Harvey. I'm going on a trip with him tomorrow.'

'Mm. As I thought.' Philip stood up. 'This definitely calls for higher authority than I can find in Colchester. Now,' he turned to Jan, 'I shall be in London for several days, but before I go — this afternoon, in fact, I'll take you visiting, Jan. I think I know someone who might be able to shed some light on this business of your family. If anyone knows anything, it'll be my Aunt Abigail. Can you get away from the "Pipe and Jar" this afternoon?'

'Oh, yes. Silas always has a nap in the afternoon. Anyway, Emily is a good friend, she'll make excuses for me.'

'Good. I'll see you this afternoon.'

Philip's Aunt Abigail was a fearsome lady, not much taller than Jan, with eyes like little black beads in a face that was all wrinkled and looked as if it had been squashed in order to make her nose touch her chin but hadn't quite succeeded.

She ordered Philip about as if he was a little boy, and to Jan's amusement Philip obeyed her without question. She really was a fearsome bundle of fine clothes.

But gradually, as he sat nervously on the edge of his stool and nibbled the oat cake that Aunt Abigail had ordered him to eat, Jan noticed the twinkle in her beady eye and could see the affection between the big, handsome sailor and his wizened old aunt.

'Well, Philip?' She chewed her gums. 'And what do you want? You never come to see me unless you want something, do you?'

'I've come for your delicious oat cake, Aunt.' Philip reached over and helped himself to another one.

'Is that all? Aren't you even going to enquire how my plaguey stiff joints are today?'

'I don't need to. I can see you're bursting with health and vitality, Aunt.' Philip winked at Jan.

'Bah!' The old lady thumped her stick on the floor. 'Well, are you going to tell me what you've come for, or am I going to leave you to eat my oat cakes and go for my rest?'

'All right, Aunt.' Philip smiled at her. He knew she loved these little mysteries. 'I'll tell you. You see my little friend here? He thinks he's the grandson of Sir Joshua Rawlings.'

'Oh, does he, indeed?' Aunt Abigail leaned forward. 'Come here, boy.' She beckoned with a bony finger so heavy with rings that Jan wondered how she'd got the strength to lift it.

'It was very sad,' she said. 'Poor Joshua. He doted on his children, you know. After the boy was thrown from his horse and killed he lavished everything on his daughter. And then when she went away — well, poor man, it nearly killed him. Wouldn't have her room touched, kept everything just as it was. And still does, to this day, for all I know. Closer, boy, closer.' She got hold of Jan and pulled him until he was right under her nose and he could smell the lavender she kept in her clothes.

'By the good Saint Christopher,' she said, 'you could be young Richard come back to life. Who do you say you are, boy?'

'I think my mother is Sir Joshua's daughter, my lady,' Jan said. He was half afraid of this fearsome little creature.

'I think you're very likely to be right,' my boy.' The old lady nodded. She looked up at Philip. 'Why? Doesn't Joshua want to own him? Has that ne'er-do-well of a godson managed to persuade him to leave everything to him already?'

'Sir Joshua hasn't even met Jan,' Philip said. 'He's away in London. But you're right, his godson tried to tell us that Sir Joshua never had a daughter.'

'That godson's a wastrel. He's already gone through his father's fortune, after worrying the poor man into his grave, and now he's after Joshua's money. And he, poor man, is so lonely, with all his family gone, that he can't see what the young rascal's up to.' Aunt Abigail snorted. 'And as for Joshua never having a daughter, why, of course he did. Pretty little thing she was, too.' She gave a wicked little smile. 'I must say I admired her for having the courage to go off with her Dutchman, they made a handsome pair. I always felt that Joshua was a bit hard on them, although I felt sorry for him.'

'Then . . .?' Jan couldn't finish what he wanted to say.

'That's right.' Philip ruffled Jan's hair. 'It looks as if you'll soon come face to face with your grandfather, my lad. I'll find Sir Joshua while I'm in London and tell him about you.'

'And please ask him if he can help me to rescue my mother and Betkin. That's the important thing. That's why I'm so anxious to find him.' Jan put his hand to his throat.

'Perhaps you'd better take him this. He might recognise it and then he'll know it's not all a mistake.' With trembling fingers Jan unfastened his lucky medallion. He still couldn't believe that after all this time things might be going right for him.

'What's that? What's that?' Aunt Abigail put out a claw and snatched it from him. 'Recognise it? I should think he will. It belonged to young Richard. It was one of Joshua's old cloth seals and Richard always wore it round his neck. Except the day of the accident. That day he'd left it at home' She gave it to Philip. 'Yes. Take it and show him. Joshua won't need anything else to convince him.'

Philip put the medallion in his pocket. 'Come along then, lad. That may be one little mystery on the way to being cleared up but there are other, and as far as I'm concerned, even more pressing matters to be attended to.'

106

THE HOUSE IN ANGEL LANE

Philip was gone for nearly a week. Jan didn't know how to contain his excitement, and with Nick away on Captain Harvey's boat it seemed the longest week of his life.

But at last Nick returned and the next day Philip came to the cabin.

'Has anything happened while I've been away?' he asked, looking from Nick to Jan and back again.

'Not a thing,' Jan said with a sigh. 'The most exciting thing was when Silas tried to sell a rotten pie to Colonel Martin of the Militia. He ought to have known better than to try it, specially on someone from the Militia.'

'What happened?' Nick asked.

'Oh, he managed to convince the colonel it was all a mistake, lying old toad,' Jan said, showing his feelings towards the landlord of the "Pipe and Jar". 'But never mind that. What about my grandfather, Philip? Have you found him? Where is he? When can I see him? Will he pay for me to go and fetch my mother and sister over to England?'

Philip held up his hand. 'One question at a time, for goodness sake.'

'Throw him in the river. That'll calm him down a bit,' Nick said, good-naturedly.

Philip laughed and perched himself on the edge of Nick's table. 'Now, Jan. I'll tell you about your grandfather and then we'll get on to more important things.'

'There *isn't* anything more important,' Jan insisted.

'That's a matter of opinion.' Philip shifted his position slightly. 'I've seen Sir Joshua Rawlings — your grandfather, Jan — and he's delighted to think he's got a grandson. I told him your story, which he believed straightaway, but when I showed him your medallion — which, incidentally, he kept — he said there could be no possible shadow of doubt that you belonged to his family. Unfortunately, he can't come back to Colchester for a few days because he's in bed with a bad leg, but when I left he'd called the physician in to bleed and purge him and he hoped he'd be well enough to come home very soon. So that's that.'

On hearing this Jan began to leap about the little cabin, squealing with excitement. He didn't know how to contain himself he was so overjoyed.

'I said we should throw him in the river, didn't I?' Nick said, narrowly escaping being strangled in one of Jan's over-exuberant bear-hugs.

'I think we shall have to if he doesn't stop this mad careering about. Hey, mind my foot.' Philip caught him as he would have attempted a cartwheel. 'Now, to other, more serious matters.' He brushed Jan and himself down and went on. 'I've been to My Lords in London and told them my suspicions. I've told them that van Migrode is mixed up in smuggling, pirating and sending escaped refugees back to Holland. I've also told them that I know he isn't actually the head of the organisation. He's pretty near the top, no doubt, but he isn't the brains behind it all.'

'Do you know who is?' Nick asked, his eyes wide.

'I've a good idea. But I need proof. And that's where you come in, Jan.'

Jan had been sitting on Nick's bed of sacks, exhausted by all his leaping about. Now he stood up. 'What do you want me to do?'

Philip took a deep breath. 'Listen carefully. I've discovered that the congregation of the Dutch Church in London have raised a lot of money, in gold, to be sent over to help the Prince of Orange in his fight against Spain. And this money has got to be shipped over to Holland. Now, what I want you to do, Jan, is to tell Mynheer van Migrode this. Tell him you think it's going to be sent from Colchester, but you don't know when, nor do you know which boat it will be on. Do you understand?'

Jan nodded, serious now, his eyes never leaving Philip's face.

'I'll come and see you in a couple of days. You should have passed the message on by that time, shouldn't you?'

'Oh, yes. Old Yellow Fangs'll probably be into the "Pipe and Jar" later today.'

Jan delivered the message to Mynheer van Migrode in amongst a lot of rubbish that he made up as he went along. That this could be a dangerous thing to do didn't occur to him in his general excitement about his grandfather. He promised the Dutchman faithfully that as soon as he found out which boat the gold would be on and when it would sail he would let him know.

'Bring the news to my house, if necessary, my boy. But come by night in that case. I don't wish you to be seen coming there.' Van Migrode smiled his yellow smile and patted Jan's head.

'Good,' Philip said, when Jan reported back to him two days later. 'Now, you can go and tell him that it's all arranged for Tuesday night and that the gold will be carried on the *Brave Endeavour*. Got that?'

'The gold will go out on the *Brave Endeavour* on Tuesday night.'

'Good boy. When will you tell him?'

'I'll go to his house tonight. That's what he said I should do.'

'I'll come with you,' Nick said at once.

'No, better not. Old Yellow Fangs might smell a rat. He thinks I work alone.'

'I hope you soon won't have to work at all,' Philip said with a sigh.

It was late when Jan made his way to Mynheer van Migrode's house. He'd had to wait until Silas was snoring in his four-poster before he crept downstairs and out of the "Pipe and Jar". The night was warm and starlit and there were a few people, beggars and vagrants mostly, to be avoided, but before long Jan was tapping on the door of the house in Angel Lane.

A servant holding a candle high let him in and showed him into a book-lined room, with candles in sconces at intervals round the walls.

Soon Abraham van Migrode came in. Jan was surprised to see that he was still fully clothed. 'Well, boy?' He held his candle high, nearly singeing his wispy black hair, and throwing long shadows on his face, giving him the appearance of an evil grey bird with a hooked beak.

Nervously, Jan delivered his message.

Van Migrode smiled and patted Jan's head. 'Good boy. Good boy,' he said. 'Now, run home fast. And tell no one you've been here.' He turned to open the door but before he could lift the latch it was opened from the other side and a tall, thin figure with bushy eyebrows and a broken nose entered.

Jan turned pale. It was the Voice.

'What's he doing here?' the newcomer snapped.

'He's brought me a message, Wouter. He's my little secret messenger boy,' van Migrode patted Jan on the head again and smiled his yellow smile.

'*Your* secret messenger boy! He's one of those boys I saw down the river. They ran our boat aground. I told you about it.'

'It was an accident,' Jan said desperately. 'We didn't mean to.'

'No, I'm sure they didn't mean to, Wouter,' van Migrode said, trying to calm the other man.

'Why were they there, then, if they weren't spying?'

110

'Spying?' Jan tried to sound innocent. 'Why should we be spying? We were looking for gulls' eggs.'

The man named Wouter leaned over to van Migrode. 'They had a telescope. They were spying. And they may have seen more than was good for them,' Jan heard him say. 'I think he should be got rid of.'

'No,' van Migrode said firmly. 'That I will not agree to. The boy has served me well.'

'The Big Master won't be pleased if there are any hitches,' Wouter warned.

'That's true.'

Jan looked from old Yellow Fangs to Wouter and back again. It was evident from their conversation that there was someone else giving the orders in the organisation, someone Wouter had just referred to as 'The Big Master'. Jan made a mental note to pass this information on to Philip when he saw him. *If* he ever saw him again. At that thought a spasm of fear clutched his heart.

There was only one door and the two men were standing by it so there was no question of Jan trying to make a dash for it. He waited, cold with fear, to see what was going to happen.

'Lock him up,' van Migrode said. 'Lock him up where he can't do any harm till all this is over. But I won't have him killed.'

'Come along, then, my fine friend.' Jan's blood ran cold at these words. He'd heard them several times but he had never thought they might actually be said to him.

The man called Wouter got hold of him by the ear and led him away.

'Now, no violence, remember,' van Migrode called after them. For once, Jan looked on him as almost an ally.

Wouter took Jan along a dark passage towards some stairs. Jan didn't have time to wonder whether he would be taken up or down — the stairs went in both directions — before he was pushed down dusty steps and thrown into a cellar. Then he heard the sound of iron bolts being shot and Wouter's footsteps retreating up the stairs.

111

It took a little while for his eyes to become accustomed to the darkness. Over in the corner he heard rustling and scurrying noises which he knew must be rats. Trying not to think about them he made his way round the wall to where what light there was from the moon came through a grating near the ceiling. The room was very low and he could easily get his fingers round the iron bars, but when he shook them they were as firm as a rock. There was no chance of removing them to make his escape and, anyway, the grating was too narrow to squeeze through.

A rat ran over his foot.

Jan was frightened. Very frightened. Here he was, imprisoned in a rat-infested cellar, with no means of escape. And no hope of rescue. He knew very well that as far as the voice-man, Wouter, was concerned, he could stay here until he rotted. Van Migrode might remember him, it seemed that he had got at least some spark of humanity, unlike his confederate, but Jan didn't hold out very much hope. He leaned back against the wall. It was cold stone and running with water. Never had he felt so alone and frightened.

He edged his way round to the grating again. Angel Lane was a narrow street, perhaps when daylight came he would be able to call for help from a passer-by. He shook the grating again. It was quite firm. He turned away.

Then the little square of grey light that had come through the grating disappeared, as if something had been placed over it, and a voice said, 'Jan! Are you there, Jan?'

It was Nick's voice.

With something approaching a sob of relief Jan ran back to the grating. He could just make out the oval of Nick's face. 'Yes, I'm locked in this cellar. And there's rats ... How did you know?'

'I followed you. But never mind that now. I've got to get you out. What's it like in there?'

'Cold and wet and there's rats ...'

'I don't mean the cellar. I mean the house.'

'A long passage runs from the door to the stairs at the end.

There are rooms off from the passage. This cellar is at the bottom of the stairs. I don't know what it's like upstairs.'

'Much the same, I expect.' Nick paused and looked round. 'The house opposite is empty,' he said, after a minute. 'If I can get in there and go upstairs I can probably climb over into this house. You could easily shake hands across from one side of the street to the other from the bedrooms.'

'Be careful, Jan warned. 'You could find yourself in old Yellow Fangs' bedroom.'

'I hope not.' Nick shuddered. 'Anyway, I'll give it a try. If it works I'll have you out of there in no time.'

In fact it was nearly an hour before Jan heard the sound of bolts being drawn back and Nick poked his head in the cellar door.

'Quick,' he said, 'and don't make a sound.'

Jan slipped out and they closed the door and shot the bolts. 'Take your shoes off in case you leave wet footprints,' Nick whispered.

Together they crept up the stairs and along the passage to the door. Slowly, Nick drew these bolts and lifted the latch. The boys stepped out into the cool night air.

Then disaster struck.

As they went to close the door it was taken by a gust of wind and slammed with a bang that was enough to waken the dead, let alone Mynheer van Migrode. Almost at once, his head, complete with nightcap, was poked out of an upstairs window.

'Who's there?' he shouted. 'What's going on?' Then catching sight of the two boys racing up the road towards the market place, 'Stop! Thief! Stop! Thief!'

'This way,' Nick panted as he led the way across the market place, through Pelham's Lane, along Trinity Street and down the steps at the Scheregate. Then, skirting the grounds of the ruined St John's Abbey to Magdalen Street, they ran down the hill to the docks. They didn't stop running until they were in Nick's cabin, and they'd been careful to reach that by Nick's secret entrance.

113

Nick halved his bed of sacks and they both lay down, completely exhausted. But they didn't sleep. Every little noise, the creak of a board, the sighs and strains of the ships tied up at the dockside that they normally didn't even notice, had them sitting up and clinging together in terror.

It was daylight before they could begin to talk naturally. And it was then that Nick related how he had got into the empty house through a broken lattice and climbed from the bedroom across to van Migrode's house.

'It might not look far when you look up at it from the ground,' he said, 'but it was a long way when it came to getting across. I had to jump! And when I landed I found myself in a bedroom with somebody snoring behind the bed curtains! I waited ages before I dared to move again because when I landed I'd knocked a candlestick over. Whew!' He shivered as he relived the experience. 'It was a nasty moment, I can tell you. Anyway, when I found the courage I crept out of the room and down the stairs and the rest you know.'

'Who was asleep in the bed?'

'I don't know. You don't think I went in and had a look, do you?'

'How did you know I was locked up there?'

'Well, I knew you were going there tonight so I hung about to watch you go. I realised you were quite right in saying you must go alone but I didn't see any harm in following you. Well, you were in there such ages that I knew something must be wrong so I had a prowl round to see what I could find out. Then I saw your fingers round the grating so I knew where you were. Then the only thing to do was to get you out.'

Jan shuddered. 'I'm glad you did. It was horrible in that cellar. It was full of rats.'

Nick got up and went to his hutch. There was a crust of bread and some stale cheese in it. That was all. He broke it equally and gave half to Jan.

'That's all the food I've got,' he said. They munched it slowly. It wasn't very nice. After a while Nick said, 'I think you'd better

114

stay here and not move outside. Van Migrode is bound to go to the "Pipe and Jar" to ask Silas about you. It'll be best if you've disappeared completely. I'll put the bucket out so that Philip will come.'

'Turn it upside down so that he comes soon. This bread and cheese won't last long and I'm hungry,' Jan said.

'I'll go and get some food from the market,' Nick said.

'No. I don't think you should go out, either. People won't question the fact that you're away because you often go with Captain Harvey.'

'Yes, you're probably right. If nobody sees me they can't ask me where you are, can they?' He picked up the bucket and tipped the water from it into an old stone jar. Then he turned the bucket upside down outside the door at the top of the steps. 'And Captain Harvey's boat's away, anyway, down at Brightlingsea, having some rotten timbers replaced, so it'll work out well.'

The boys waited. All day they waited, their bellies rumbling with hunger. In desperation Nick went to find food when it got dark and came back with stale pies from the pastry-cook's. But still Philip didn't come.

For two days they waited, living on what Nick could find on his nocturnal trips, becoming more and more anxious. Monday came, still with no sign of Philip. By Tuesday they were getting really anxious.

'The gold will be on the *Brave Endeavour* tonight,' Jan said, repeating the message he had given van Migrode.

'I wonder if something may have gone wrong,' Nick said, with a worried frown. 'Maybe Philip has had other things to worry about, so he hasn't had time to come with us.'

'What do you mean?' Jan looked up from the rope Nick had been teaching him to splice to relieve the boredom.

'Well, I wasn't going to say anything, but I know he's been in Colchester.'

'How do you know that?' Jan said quickly.

'Because he had dinner at Sir John Dalrymple's house the

115

other night. I saw him and several other people leaving when I was out looking for food.'

'What other people?'

'Oh, I don't know. Most of them I didn't even recognise. There was somebody called Rupert, I think. I heard someone say, "Goodnight, Rupert".'

'That's Sir John's nephew. I met him at my grandfather's house.' Jan thought for a bit. 'You'd have thought Philip would have spared us a few minutes, wouldn't you? Oh!' he threw down the rope he had been splicing, 'I wish I knew what was going on. I hate being shut up here.'

'Well, I can assure you that this is the safest place for you to be. Van Migrode is out for your blood and making no secret of the fact.'

It was Philip who had spoken. He had come in through the secret way so silently that neither of the boys had heard him enter.

BATTLE AT SEA

The boys both turned at Philip's voice. He was wearing smart clothes but he looked tired and travel-weary as he slumped down on to the stool by the table.

'Now,' he said, 'what have you been up to to set van Migrode screaming after your blood? I guessed you'd be holed up here and quite safe, so I haven't been too worried about you. But I came as soon as I could.'

Quickly, the boys told him their tale; of Jan's imprisonment after delivering the message and how Nick had helped him escape.

'Do you think van Migrode believed what you told him?' Philip asked, when they had finished.

'Yes, I think so,' Jan said doubtfully. 'But Wouter, the man we called the Voice, didn't trust me at all. He remembered seeing me out on the river. By this time he's probably convinced Yellow Fangs that I'm a traitor.'

'It certainly sounds like it from the hue and cry that's going on in a quiet, underground sort of way,' Philip said. He looked at them both. 'I think,' he said, after a moment's silence, 'I think I'd better take you with me. While I can't promise that you'll be exactly safe where we're going, at least you'll be out of the clutches of those ruffians and their henchmen.'

'Where are you going?' Nick asked. 'Are you going with the *Brave Endeavour*, to see that the gold gets there safely?'

A strange expression crossed Philip's face; one that neither of the boys could understand. 'No,' he said. 'I'm not going on the *Brave Endeavour*. I'm going out with Captain Harvey on the *Mimosa*. And I'm going to take you with me. I'll be back for you in half an hour.'

The boys had nothing to do but wait and speculate until Philip returned and hurried them away from Colchester in a fast coach.

'Where are you taking us?' they asked.

'To Brightlingsea.' Philip would tell them nothing more.

Captain Harvey's ship looked as if it had had a complete refit. Her topsides gleamed and her hull had been freshly tarred. No sooner had the long boat taken them aboard than the order was given to make sail and the ship nosed out of the mouth of the estuary.

Jan and Nick had been taken down to Captain Harvey's cabin and told to stay there. Nick had been here many times. Situated in the sterncastle it stretched the width of the boat, its windows looking out over the stern. Below the windows was Captain Harvey's bed; his desk, with all its charts, was in the middle of the cabin and a lantern swung over it. But there was something different today and for a moment Nick couldn't think what it was. Then he realised. There were two large box-like things, one either side of the cabin, covered in canvas.

Gingerly, he lifted a corner of the canvas and then gave a gasp. 'Jan!' he cried. 'They're guns!'

After the first shock of their discovery the two boys sat down to discuss what they had found.

'Captain Harvey's boat's never been armed before,' Nick said excitedly.

'There seem to be an awful lot of people on board, too,' Jan said.

'This is what must have been happening when Captain Harvey said he was having rotten timbers replaced,' Nick decided.

The door opened and Philip came in. He held up his hand for silence as the boys began to question him. 'Wait. I'm going to tell you,' he said.

The boys quietened immediately; they could see how tired and anxious their friend looked.

'You know that I've suspected there was somebody at the head of this organisation? Somebody above van Migrode and the Voice?'

The boys nodded. 'I heard Yellow Fangs and the Voice talk about "The Big Master",' Jan said.

'That proves I was right,' Philip nodded. 'Not that I needed proof of that. What I need to prove is who this "Big Master" is. I've had my suspicions for some time but so far he's been too clever to get caught. So I've set up a trap.' He looked hard at Jan. 'You told van Migrode the gold would be aboard the *Brave Endeavour*, didn't you?'

'Yes.' Jan didn't take his eyes off Philip's face.

'Well, *I've* let it be known in what I think are the right quarters, that the gold has secretly been transferred to the *Mimosa*.'

'And has it?' Nick asked, his eyes wide. 'Is that why the guns are on board?'

'The gold has never been anywhere near Colchester,' Philip said with a smile. 'It was shipped from Sandwich this morning. In broad daylight.'

Nick frowned. 'So what . . .?'

'If we arrive safely in Holland and no questions asked, we shall know that I've made a mistake and that I'll have to think again.'

'And if not?' Jan asked.

'If not, we could have quite a bloody battle, I fear.'

'What do you think he meant, have quite a bloody battle?' Nick asked, when Philip had left them.

'Well, I suppose, *if* Philip has told the right person, he will order the gold to be be removed from this boat,' Jan said, frowning.

'So, if this boat is attacked, Philip will know he was right and that he told this "Big Master", whoever he is.' Nick looked at the canvas-covered guns. 'And that's what they've been put in for. Captain Harvey wasn't having rotten timbers replaced at all, he was having these guns installed.'

They had no further chance to talk because the ship was now a hive of activity. Captain Harvey came to his cabin and Philip followed him.

'I don't like it, Lieutenant,' the Captain said, 'I know I agreed to let you do it, but my ship wasn't built to carry guns like this, nor an extra complement of navy men. I only hope she'll stand up to it.'

'She had the extra timbers put in to strengthen her?'

'Oh, yes. Everything was done according to the specifications.'

'Then everything should be all right.'

Food was brought, salt pork and ale. Philip and the Captain ate theirs with relish and so did Nick, but Jan found he wasn't hungry. He hoped he wasn't going to be sick.

It was getting dusk when the lookout sighted something coming up fast on the starboard bow. Quietly, orders were given to make ready the guns and suddenly the whole ship was busy with naval men running to their stations and preparing the guns that had been secretly installed, their muzzles only inches behind the new tarred canvas gunports.

'You two lads, you can make yourselves useful as messengers,' Captain Harvey said. 'You, Dutch boy, run to Lieutenant Jardine and ask him to come to my cabin.'

Jan ran off. He wasn't sure where he was going but he picked his way among the men, busy at their posts, until he reached Philip.

'I think if we can keep our nerve and let them get the grapnels in before we open fire we'll stand a better chance of getting them,' Philip said when he returned with Jan.

'You're sure we're not being approached by those brigands, the Sea Beggars?' Captain Harvey said, training his telescope on the approaching boat. 'I've no wish to hand my boat over to those pirates on a plate.'

'I think not, Captain. That boat is the *Thetis*. I can see by her unusual shape and long bowsprit. I think you'll find Mynheer van Migrode training his eye-glass on us, just as carefully as we are on them. The crew is acting quite normally up on deck? We don't want anything to arouse suspicion.'

'Absolutely. They've been ordered to carry out the watch as normal. But they're not happy, Lieutenant, I can tell you that. And with what looks very much like a pirate ship bearing down on us, who can blame them? I'm not exactly dancing with joy myself.'

He put his telescope to his eye again, just as the *Thetis* fired a shot across the bows of the *Mimosa*.

'Heave to,' Captain Harvey gave the order and there was the creak of timbers as the ship answered the pull of the sheets.

A moment later there was the whine of ropes as grapnels snaked across from the *Thetis*, digging into the *Mimosa*'s rigging and holding the boats firmly together.

'Hold your fire, let them get close,' the order had gone quietly through the ship. Now, the order rang through loud and clear, 'FIRE!'

The gunports opened and the whole ship shuddered and lurched as the six guns spoke as one with a deafening roar. When the smoke cleared the *Thetis* could be seen listing heavily from a great gaping hole in her side, one mast tilted at a crazy angle, and sails dangling like rags from the spars. Caught completely by surprise, she managed to fire a few sporadic shots in reply but they were largely ineffectual and only one or two hit their mark.

The small swivel guns mounted on the fore and sterncastle of the *Mimosa* rapped out, shredding what was left of the *Thetis*'s sails and scattering the men on deck. Fire had already begun licking the rigging.

'Cut those grapnel lines,' Captain Harvey ordered. 'And bear away. That boat'll be nothing more than a fire ship in seconds. Jump about there! Look lively!'

Nick and Jan ran to and fro clearing wreckage and helping to get the wounded below. Out of the corner of his eye Jan thought he saw Yellow Fangs, standing on deck, surrounded by flames, beside himself with fear and fury, shouting orders that nobody was listening to in the panic to get off the burning ship.

'A bag of gold to the man who kills that yellow-haired boy!' he screamed, pointing at Jan.

He was like a madman and Jan was glad of the expanse of water, small though it was, that separated the two ships. Then, as Jan watched, a spar, trailing smoke and flames from what was left of sails and rigging, crashed to the deck where Yellow Fangs was standing. He would never scream again.

'I said, get those lines cut!' Captain Harvey's voice was like a whiplash, as sailors hacked away with axes at the grapnel lines that were still keeping the two ships from parting. The last of them snapped.

'Harden sail!' There was the creak of rigging as the sheets were pulled in and the *Mimosa* drew away from the burning *Thetis*, now well alight and listing heavily. Jan saw a few figures jump or fall into the sea and then, with a splintering crash and rumble, the *Thetis* rolled over and sank in a cloud of hissing, steaming spray.

Then silence.

All that was left of the *Thetis* were the charred and broken timbers that littered the sea all around and four heads bobbing in the water as they tried to swim to safety. A boat was lowered in an almost leisurely fashion to pick them up.

'Well, Captain, your little ship stood up to that shindig remarkably well,' Philip said, with a smile, his teeth gleaming white in his smoke-blackened face.

'Aye, you're right. And the whole business was over in less than ten minutes,' Captain Harvey said. 'It certainly took them by surprise.'

'That, of course,' Philip said wryly, 'was the whole idea.'

The four survivors from the *Thetis* were hauled aboard and hurried below to be clapped in irons till they could be dealt with ashore.

One of them was Wouter, the Voice. He looked at Jan with an expression of venomous hatred as he was rough-handled along the companion-way.

Even in captivity that man could send shivers of fear down Jan's spine and he put up his hand to his forehead where he could feel cold sweat trickling down. But when he looked, it wasn't sweat at all. His hand was red with blood.

He stared at it for a moment and then everything went black and he sank to the deck, unconscious.

HOME AT LAST

When Jan came round he was lying in the captain's bunk and his head was swathed in bandages. Nick was sitting beside him with his arm in a sling.

'It's not fair,' Nick grumbled. 'You did at least get hurt in the battle. I tripped over a rope and fell down the companion-way when it was all over.'

'Where are we going now?' Jan struggled to sit up.

'We're on our way back to Colchester. In fact, we'll be tying up in *Mimosa*'s berth in about five minutes.'

'I suppose we'll never know who the "Big Master" was, now,' Jan said thoughtfully. 'I suppose he sank with the ship.'

'Yes,' Nick said, 'I s'pose he did. But as long as he's out of the way it doesn't much matter, does it? At least he can't do any more harm.'

'I would have liked to know, all the same,' Jan said.

Nick looked out of the window. 'We're nearly there. Do you think you can walk?'

'Of course I can walk!' Jan said crossly. His head felt a bit heavy but he was sure it was all the silly cloth they'd wrapped round it that was making it throb so. He got to his feet, steadying himself against the desk, and together the two boys went up on deck. As they stood watching the familiar jumble of cargoes being loaded and unloaded on the quayside Philip came over to them.

'Oh,' he said, with a grin, 'I see we've got a couple of walking wounded.' His face was black with smoke and his clothes were torn and dirty. 'Now, you're to stay aboard here, with Captain Harvey, until I come for you. I'll be as quick as I can.'

While he was gone Captain Harvey had hot water brought to his cabin and the boys were put in a big wooden tub and bathed, helped because of their injuries by a beefy midshipman. When they were dried they were given clean clothes, the like of which Nick had never worn in his life before, made of soft velvet and fine linen, with fancy leather shoes.

When Philip came back he wouldn't have recognised them but for their bandages.

'Now,' he said, 'to Boxted and your grandfather, Jan.'

They drove to Boxted in a coach, together with Captain Harvey and the beefy midshipman. When they arrived they were shown into a small library off the big hall. An elderly gentleman, with a round face and tufty grey hair, was sitting in a big chair with his leg propped up on a stool. His godson, Rupert, was with him and so was Sir John Dalrymple, Rupert's uncle.

Old Sir Joshua held out his hand to Jan and Jan went over to him without a word. The old man looked at him for a moment. Then he said gruffly, 'Took you long enough to find me, didn't it, boy? What've you been doing all this time?' But although his voice was gruff he blew his nose very hard and he had to turn his head so that Jan shouldn't see him wipe a tear from his eye.

'Please, sir,' Jan said anxiously, 'I don't mind what you do with me, but will you help my mother and sister to come to England?'

Sir Joshua patted his arm and looked at him with kind brown eyes. 'Never fear, my boy. Your mother and sister are quite safe. In fact, I shouldn't be surprised if the ship bringing them over

125

from Holland is waiting off Harwich to come in with the tide.' He turned to Rupert. 'I thought my daughter was lost to me for ever, my boy. And now I find that not only is she coming back to me but that I have two grandchildren as well — and one of them as brave a lad as ever sat in a pair of breeches.' He smiled at Jan. 'I'm sure you rejoice with me, Rupert, my boy.'

'Yes, of course, godfather,' Rupert said, stiffly, but his face was ugly with jealousy.

Sir John Dalrymple stepped forward. 'This is indeed a time for celebration. Not only has Sir Joshua found his family again, but we must congratulate our friends, Captain Harvey and Lieutenant Jardine, on fighting off the Sea Beggars and getting safely back to port.' He lowered his voice. 'Is the gold safe, Jardine?' he asked in an undertone.

'Quite safe, Sir John,' Philip said, in his normal tone. 'It was shipped out from Sandwich yesterday.'

'Sandwich?' Sir John said, astonished. Then, quickly, he recovered himself. 'Ah, good.' He nodded his head several times.

'And they weren't Sea Beggars that we fought off, they were *your* men, Sir John.'

'My men? What do you mean, my men?' Sir John's red face turned bright purple and Jan watched anxiously, afraid it might burst.

'I mean Mynheer van Migrode and the man called Wouter, among others,' Philip said.

'They're not *my* men! What have they got to do with me?'

'They've been working for you, Sir John. *You* were the "Big Master". I suspected it when the landlord of the "Woolpack" was murdered along with his wife and ostler. I'd come to you for a warrant to arrest them, so you knew what I planned to do. But you couldn't allow that, could you, in case they talked. So they had to be silenced.'

'I thought Wouter had killed them,' Nick broke in. He had been silent up till now, standing by the door, a little apart from everyone else.

'Yes, and so it might have been,' Philip agreed. 'And that was

126

why I wasn't absolutely sure, although I suspected Sir John. But I needed real proof. And now I've got it.'

'You can't prove *anything*,' Sir John snapped.

'It's proof enough that you were the only person who knew the "gold" — which wasn't gold at all, but boxes of useless junk — was being transferred from the *Brave Endeavour* to the *Mimosa. Nobody else knew.* Why would the *Mimosa* have been attacked if someone hadn't been told it had valuables on it? Oh,' Philip held up his hand as Sir John began to bluster, 'it's no good trying to deny it. Your henchman, Wouter, has already told us everything we need to know. Enough and more to get you hanged, drawn and quartered before the biggest crowd Colchester has ever seen.' He nodded to Captain Harvey and the beefy midshipman, who were standing just behind Sir John. Before he knew what was happening they had taken an arm each and were holding him fast. 'One moment,' Philip said, 'before taking him away. Why did you do it, Sir John?'

'Why do you think?' Sir John said, with something approaching a snarl. 'I did it because there was money in it, of course.'

Philip gave him a look of utter contempt. 'Just as I thought,' he said in disgust. He nodded to Captain Harvey. 'Take him to the Castle.'

Captain Harvey and the midshipman dragged Sir John away to the Castle, the great fortress that had stood overlooking the town for five hundred years, where the prisons were the strongest for miles around. Rupert, Sir John's nephew, followed. 'I'll come and see you when you're in prison, Uncle. I'll look after your house for you. Remember, I'm your only living relative . . .' they heard him saying as he went.

'That was a smart piece of work, Jardine,' Sir Joshua said. He looked past Philip to Nick, who was still standing alone near the door. 'And who is this young man?'

Jan went over to him. 'This is Nick. He's my friend.' And Jan told his grandfather of all they had been through together.

'And you live in a *cabin*! A cabin you've made yourself in the corner of a sailmaker's shed?'

127

'They don't mind,' Nick said quickly. 'The sailmaker said I could live there.'

'And you want to be a sailor?'

'Yes, in the Queen's Navy,' Nick said proudly.

'Hm. You ought to go to school, then,' the old man said sternly.

Nick's face fell. 'I did go to school once, but my gran couldn't afford to keep me there so I had to leave,' he said sadly.

'Well, I'd better see to it that you go back there, hadn't I? With Jan, here.' He turned to Jan. 'Because no grandson of mine will grow up without going to school.' He turned back to Nick. 'Would you like that, boy?'

Nick could hardly believe his ears. 'Oh, yes, sir, please, sir,' he said eagerly.

Sir Joshua cleared his throat and tried to look stern but the twinkle in his eye gave him away. 'And you can't live in a cabin in a sailmaker's loft if you go to school, can you? So you'd better come and live here with Jan. Would you like that?'

Nick found he couldn't speak because his throat had a funny lump in it. Then he managed to say, in a squeaky little voice that he didn't recognise as his own, 'Does that mean I'll sleep on a feather mattress? A *real* feather mattress?'

Everybody roared with laughter. 'I shouldn't be at all surprised if it does,' Sir Joshua said.

Jan looked at his friend and grinned. Everything had come out all right at last. In fact, more than all right, because Nick, his friend, who had played such a big part in helping him to find grandfather's house, was going to live here, too, with this gruff, lovable old man. And soon it would be time to fetch Mama and Betkin from the ship and bring them home. What more could a boy ask?

END